"YOU'RE A DEVIL SENT TO TORTURE ME, AREN'T you?" Josh asked.

Amy felt an exquisite ache of longing go through her, and caught her breath. She stayed where she was one instant longer, willing him to respond, then realized she was insane. Her gaze faltered.

"Don't go," he whispered, and pulled her slowly into his strong arms.

His gray eyes seemed to devour her, and she remembered again the determined strength with which he'd canoed across the lake. Josh Kita might be controlled and graceful with a waltz, but he restrained a savage power that lurked behind his hooded expression. The realization excited her, sending a shiver of expectation down her back.

What the hell am I doing? Josh thought, holding his desire fiercely in check. This had to be wrong. He couldn't kiss her, not the way he wanted to, when they hardly knew each other, when it was the moonlight talking and he was old enough to know better.

She began to smile that sideways smile that made it hard for him to remember he was a gentleman.

"Who are you protecting?" she asked.

"You're not supposed to read my mind," he said.

"Then stop me."

WHAT ARE *LOVESWEPT* ROMANCES?

They are stories of true romance and touching emotion. We believe those two very important ingredients are constants in our highly sensual and very believable stories in the LOVE-SWEPT line. Our goal is to give you, the reader, stories of consistently high quality that may sometimes make you laugh, sometimes make you cry, but are always fresh and creative and contain many delightful surprises within their pages.

Most romance fans read an enormous number of books. Those they truly love, they keep. Others may be traded with friends and soon forgotten. We hope that each LOVESWEPT romance will be a treasure—a "keeper." We will always try to publish

LOVE STORIES YOU'LL NEVER FORGET
BY AUTHORS YOU'LL ALWAYS REMEMBER

The Editors

Loveswept® 887

NORTH STAR RISING

CARAGH O'BRIEN

BANTAM BOOKS
NEW YORK · TORONTO · LONDON · SYDNEY · AUCKLAND

NORTH STAR RISING

A Bantam Book / May 1998

ISBN 0-553-44635-5

Published simultaneously in the United States and Canada

PRINTED IN THE UNITED STATES OF AMERICA

OPM   10 9 8 7 6 5 4 3 2 1

For Nancy R. E. O'Brien

ONE

Amy leaned her elbows on the balcony railing and eased her pinched toes out of the high heels, half wishing she could hurl the shoes into the lake. "Oh, for a pair of hiking boots," she muttered. Through the open French doors behind her, she could hear the other bridesmaids laughing at something Briana was saying, and the musical sound made her smile, despite her sore toes.

Before her, the pearly water of Lake Eloise in Darwin, Montana, stretched out between a deep cut of mountains and ended in a distant white shelf of glacier. Three clouds hung in the sky as if an artist had launched giant cotton balls to see how the shadows would look on the mountains. In one shadow, Château Lake Eloise graced the northern shore of the lake, an elegant old-fashioned stone hotel with other balconies like hers and an expansive store terrace below. In another hour the wedding would take place in the ballroom that opened onto the same terrace, and hotel workers were already arranging groups of chairs. Amy breathed in the cool May air, trying to absorb the beauty and enchantment of the morning, when another burst of laughter erupted.

She turned carefully in her nylons and peered back into the salon where the bride and the three other bridesmaids were trying to get Briana's strapless bra to fit under her wedding dress. There was a knock at the door, and Briana, prim-faced, made a classic cross-your-heart gesture over her chest.

One woman peeped out the doorway. "It's the photographer!"

The women laughed again.

"Send him away!"

"Bring him in!"

Briana shrieked.

Amy grinned and edged a bit farther along the balcony, out of view. She wasn't exactly hiding. She would go in as soon as they needed her, but she'd only get in the way now. Besides, she'd had a whole morning of makeup and nylons and a dress that fit so snugly around her breasts and waist that she could swear every contour of her body was exposed. She couldn't get used to the way it felt—like a bathing suit, but clingy instead of stretchy. The other women didn't seem to mind the fuss. On the contrary, they obviously relished the transformation, dancing forward and backward in front of the big mirror and lavishing each other with compliments. Amy had already been called ravishing, wicked, and tubular. Like a regular tsunami, she thought.

For Briana's sake, Amy could submit to the ultrafeminine look. But she felt like an impostor in the mascara and blush, the lipstick that matched that of the other bridesmaids. A hairdresser had styled her blond hair, sweeping it upward, adding fake pearls, and spraying it until she had a helmet head, when what she really longed to do on a morning like this, in a place like this, was to go hiking. Or better yet . . . She scanned the length of the lake to where a lone canoer was deftly paddling toward the Château. "I'd be in that canoe," she said, envious.

She watched the canoer, idly at first, then with more interest, as he shot the canoe smoothly over the water. At first she thought he was sprinting for the fun of it, but as the wake extended farther and farther behind him and his arms continued to flash in a steady, lake-eating rhythm, a strange tension tightened in her body, a vicarious thread of energy. She knew perfectly well what strength it took to canoe at such a pace.

He was paddling with the force of a man facing rapids and log heads, not a serene surface of water. Either he was possessed, she thought, or he was a workout fiend. He canoed from the stern, so the bow of the boat rode slightly higher, and he'd pushed his shirtsleeves up to his elbows, revealing bare forearms that matched the color of the flashing wooden paddle. She instinctively rubbed her fingers against her palms, feeling her calluses. The man flipped his paddle from starboard to port, timing the motion with fluid grace so as not to miss a beat.

He was still well out on the lake, but in another minute he would be just below the Château. Amy was curious to see what he looked like closer up, but she calculated from the angle that she wouldn't be able to see him once he reached the rental dock. She leaned a little farther over the balcony railing, squinting.

Just then, the cloud over the Château moved away, and the shadow passed visibly across the lake and up the mountain before it was gone. Amy blinked hard against the onslaught of sunlight and lifted a hand over her eyes. When she looked down at the canoer again, the lake was almost painfully bright, dazzling in bits of reflected light that made the canoe, by contrast, a nearly black silhouette. Just beyond the balcony the canoer stopped paddling and laid the paddle across his knees, letting the canoe glide noiselessly over the brilliant water.

Amy caught her breath, struck by the sheer magnetism that emanated from the man. She could see his chest expanding with his rapid breaths, could see beads of water drop silently from his paddle to the lake. Then he looked up. He didn't scan the shoreline or the rest of the Château or the rental dock. His gaze zeroed in on her balcony, and he squinted directly at her. She knew it from the steady, unwavering angle of his head and from an elusive disturbance in her inner magnetic field.

Amy set both hands on the stone railing to steady herself. Her chiffon sleeve ruffled against her shoulder, and the breeze skimmed across her face, pulling a tendril of hair across her temple, but still she looked down, waiting for his gaze to pass on once he realized she was a stranger.

Instead, he tipped his chin up slightly and then, with subtle gallantry, he nodded a greeting.

Amy was so surprised she stared, frozen. She couldn't look away; she couldn't respond. All she could do was wait while his image seared its way into her memory: bare forearms, shock of dark hair, and the steady, restrained masculine power in the perfect balance of his canoe on the shining water. He tipped his head sideways, as if easing tension in his neck, then smiled the most arrogant, most captivating smile she'd ever seen.

"Where is she?" Briana called. "Hey, Aim. Ollie-ollie in come free."

Her heart beating erratically, Amy turned to see the bride standing in the doorway, smiling. Briana had spoken the phrase they always used to signal the end of their childhood games of hide and seek. Her white dress was a dream of satin and pearls, as dainty and warm as Briana herself, and Amy felt a surge of joy for her friend on her wedding day.

"We've mastered the bra problem," Briana said, grinning. "Time for photos."

Only then did Amy feel a full wave of jitters, and they had nothing to do with photos. She glanced back at the water, where the canoer was still watching her, as if he had known she would look one more time. She turned proudly away from the balcony and collected her shoes.

Amy swore she wouldn't make a fool of herself during the ceremony, but she cried anyway out of a mix of heady emotions—happiness for Briana, sadness at losing her favorite single friend, and some unexplained, powerful yearning that came with the haunting strains of the solo violin. When the bride and groom walked back up the aisle through the crowd of friends and relatives, Amy's eyes were so watery, she could hardly see to follow. She clung to the arm of one of the groomsmen, letting him lead her up the aisle, and she welcomed the peace of a small hallway where he stopped and discreetly offered a handkerchief. The rest of the bridal party turned right toward the terrace, but Amy hardly noticed.

With a last choking sob, she headed for the nearest

corner to blow her nose loudly into the handkerchief. A muffled laugh came from over her shoulder, and she looked up, surprised.

"Bless you," the groomsman said. He lifted one eyebrow and slid his hands into the pockets of his tuxedo trousers.

"I'm not sneezing," Amy said. "I'm bawling my eyes out."

"I know. You started sniveling halfway through the service."

Several things struck Amy at once: He was not the groomsman she'd been assigned to, he was by far the most handsome man she had ever seen, and he seemed distinctly amused by her wretchedness. Frowning, she took in the jaunty angle of his head, the lazy smile with which he watched her, and she realized he was waiting for something, some sort of recognition.

"It's you," she said, wiping away the last of her tears.

"Josh Kita," he said, nodding. "And you must be Juliet. Of balcony fame."

Amy laughed. Josh Kita was the canoer and the fourth groomsman, the one who hadn't been able to attend the rehearsal the day before. Because of their standing configuration during the ceremony, he must have been the one partially concealed by the tall arrangement of flowers around the wedding candle. Otherwise she certainly would have noticed him, even through her tears. Josh must have switched places to end up as her partner on the way out.

"Actually, my name's Amy," she said. "Amy Larkspur. And I never snivel." She looked down at the handkerchief to fold it into a square. "Tell me my mascara didn't run."

She gazed up at him trustingly, and Josh had to catch his breath.

Damn, she was pretty, he thought. Far too pretty.

When Josh had agreed to stand up for his friend Lee, he knew he'd have mixed feelings about being in a wedding, but he hadn't expected anything like this. Since his divorce five years earlier, he'd avoided weddings, partly from a superstition he'd bring the bad luck of his own marriage to the happy couple. He knew that was absurd, an excuse to avoid facing the real reason why he didn't like weddings, but nevertheless, he had deliberately steered clear of exactly this sort of situation.

It was bad enough seeing how happy Lee and Briana were. They seemed ideally suited and deliriously in love, full of a magic hopefulness that made him feel like a jerk for being envious. It was painful to recall how fleeting his own marital bliss had been, and to know what mistakes had landed him, finally, in his own private hell. While outwardly he joined in the celebration, inside he felt more isolated than he had for a long time.

What he needed was a chance to be by himself. The last few weeks hadn't given him any solitude at all, and he knew he was on edge. He'd hoped to claim an hour for himself that morning, in the canoe, but even that attempt had been foiled.

He'd seen her first as a salmon-colored speck of fluttering fabric on the balcony, a distraction that called to him when he was far out on the lake. He'd used her as a focal point for his straight-line canoeing, expecting she'd be gone by the time he made it to the Château. But she had stayed, and she'd been watching when he looked up. He'd liked the way she leaned on the railing, the squareness of her shoulders. Even from a distance he'd sensed a stubbornness in her that reminded him of Chloe, his oldest daughter, and that made him smile.

Then later he'd recognized her immediately when she came down the aisle preceding the bride, her blond head poised, her tanned hands steady on her bouquet of white roses. There was nothing dainty about those hands, and yet they were feminine in a way that puzzled and intrigued him. Staring at the bridesmaid's hands, he remembered the day he'd married Shannon, and he felt a strange, crumpling pang of regret. He'd expected regret, but what followed had shaken him more: the strong, certain feeling of forgiveness that flowed through him, as if he could finally acquit his ex-wife for all the bitterness. The forgiveness had surprised him and made him uneasy, and he'd felt it was somehow tied to the fair-haired woman with the steady hands walking under the chandelier of the ballroom toward the altar. But that was insane.

Now that same mesmerizing woman was standing before him, her huge, damp brown eyes looking expectantly up at him, and damn if he didn't want to kiss her. The tug of attraction was so foreign he almost resented it. Who was this woman? He decided to satisfy himself by using his thumb to wipe an imaginary smudge from under her left eye, but the contact with her warm skin didn't satisfy him one iota.

"You look fine," he said, his voice rougher than he'd intended.

She smiled quizzically. "Not ravishing? Not wicked?"

He frowned. "Is that what you're used to being called?"

Amy could just imagine one of her canoeing buddies

calling her "ravishing" and had to laugh. "No." She absently slipped his handkerchief into her satchel.

The tender skin below her eye was still tingling from his gentle touch, and she felt the bare skin along her neck and arms become hyperaware of how near he was. He was older than she, with strong, regular features and gray eyes that had a faintly Asian quality to them. She tried to check his ring finger, but his left hand was in his pocket.

Say something, she urged herself. But what if she said something stupid or boring? *Flirt, then.* But she didn't know how. *Then think like a bridesmaid, idiot!*

"Did you ever have to wear shoes that hurt so badly all you could think of was getting out of them?" she blurted out.

"That's what you're thinking about now?" he asked.

She nodded.

"That's all you can think of?"

She watched his eyes when he talked, liking the warm humor behind them.

"Yes."

She saw his gaze lower to her lips and linger, as if he were considering the shape outlined by her lipstick. A curious, light feeling circled in her belly. His eyes flicked back to hers, and the humor was laced with an interest that shot a bolt of response through her.

"Then take them off," he said softly.

Take *what* off? He took half a step back and smiled down at her shoes, apparently expecting her to take them off immediately.

She couldn't move. "Excuse me?"

"At least for a moment."

Feeling warmth rise up her throat, she bit her lower

lip and looked beyond him to see that the hallway had cleared and they were alone. She pulled the wide hem of her skirt back against her knees and bent to get a look at her own shoes, pretty little pumps dyed salmon to match her gown. They didn't look as if they hurt, but they were a full size too small. "What the heck," she said, and lifted one foot to wedge off the shoe.

When she lost her balance, Josh instantly put a hand out to steady her elbow.

"You know I have to put them back on before I go into the reception," she said. "Even if they *are* the wrong size. There was a mix-up with the ordering."

"Why wear them at all?"

He couldn't be serious. She smiled again, noting that with her heels off, she had to look up another inch to meet his eyes. He was tall; her chin was barely level with his broad shoulders. But her gaze was even with his mouth, and his devastatingly charming smile made half of her panic. Who *was* this guy?

"There's a dress code for bridesmaids, in case you hadn't noticed," she said, and wiggled her nyloned toes in happy relief. Putting a hand up to gingerly touch her fancy 'do, she felt that her blond curls were soft despite the hair spray, and she self-consciously turned her finger in a loose tendril at the nape of her neck. "It includes the hair, the makeup, the fantastic dress, the matching satchel, and of course, the shoes."

Before she could realize his intention, he gently tugged the shoes from her grasp.

"What if the shoes are accidentally misplaced?" he asked. "Like they were accidentally the wrong size?"

She watched in alarm as he put one of her shoes in his tuxedo coat pocket.

"You can't," she said, reaching out to reclaim the other shoe before it, too, disappeared.

He merely lifted the shoe out of reach.

"What if, instead of going into the reception, you take a walk around the corner to the gift shop with me and we buy some moccasins?" He motioned to the door that led toward the hotel lobby, clearly expecting her to come along. She peeked out at the inviting carpet for one traitorous moment before she realized she was insane to consider it.

She stood on tiptoe, glowering at him, and grabbed the shoe out of his fingers. "The other one," she said sternly, holding out her hand.

"Nice soft moccasins," he said. "One size fits all."

She refused to smile. "I have a duty. A shoe duty, and I shall not be thwarted. Give it over."

Slowly he pulled the other shoe out of his pocket and relinquished it. She steadied herself against the wall and put them both on again before he could try some other nonsense. When the back of her right shoe hit the back of her heel, she knew a blister was forming. If she didn't get a Band-Aid on it soon, she'd be limping. And for that, she blamed Josh.

He chuckled deep in his throat. "I almost had you," he said.

"You almost had my *shoe*. You're mean to tempt me with moccasins when I'm determined to look ladylike for once in my life."

As she began to walk past him, he folded his arms across his chest, still smiling.

"Next time I'll have to tempt you with something stronger."

She turned to look at him, puzzled, and the expression on his face doubled her uncertainty. He spoke as if she were the one he was after. But he wasn't anything like the other guys who ordinarily came on to her. Then again, she looked so unlike the way she usually did, she might as well be in disguise.

Hiding a smile, Amy turned away and joined the rest of the guests in the ballroom, where the chairs from the ceremony had been cleared to make room for a dance floor. With a lingering sense of relief, she noticed that sliding doors had been pulled back to reveal a sumptuous buffet, and in one corner a string quartet was playing romantic tunes from the thirties and forties. All 150 guests were dressed in tuxedos and tea-length gowns, but the formal clothes didn't seem to have an inhibiting effect at all. In fact, just the opposite was true, and lively conversations and laughter could be heard as a counterpoint to the music.

Amy liked the candles most of all. Even though it was midafternoon, candlelight created a soft glow along the smooth wood walls and beams of the rustic but elegant interior, accentuating the natural beauty of the carefully hewn wood. She felt as though she was in another time, when people lived closer to the forests and the earth, and reflected this in their homes. Through the French doors, she could see the stone terrace and the blue-green of Lake Eloise beyond. It was as if the bridal couple had brought the whole wedding party to a honeymoon spot.

Knowing Briana, Amy wasn't surprised that the wedding was perfect. They'd grown up together in Harmony, Minnesota, and even when Briana's family had moved to Montana, the two friends had stayed close through letters and phone calls. As she saw the bride in the distance, Amy felt an odd twinge of loss, and for the hundreth time she silently wished her all the best.

The reception advanced easily through hors d'oeuvres and vichyssoise to dinner, with guests proposing spontaneous toasts to the new couple. Amy talked with old friends and met others, and enjoyed herself hugely, especially after sneaking away long enough to put a Band-Aid on her heel. During Briana and Lee's first dance, a mirrored ball was lowered, scattering points of light around the room. People laughed, then sighed, and Amy decided maybe weddings weren't so corny after all.

And then, because she couldn't help herself any longer, she searched for the tall form and broad shoulders of Josh Kita, knowing he would be conspicuously taller than most of the men present. When she couldn't find Josh, she was aware of a sense of disappointment, and she gazed through the open doorways to where a violet light scattered over the lake and terrace, bringing evening. Where had he gone? And what had made her expect he would come and find her long before this?

"Care to dance?"

His voice came from behind her, a low rumble in her ear, and she turned her head to see him. His gray eyes were watchful, receptive, and she sensed something different about him.

"With you?" she asked.

He laughed quietly. "No, with Uncle George."

She glanced at the head table, where Uncle George had his leg cast propped up on a chair.

"I'd love to dance with Uncle George," she said.

"So would I, but you'll have to do." He tucked her

hand around his elbow to lead her through the tables to the dance floor.

Since her formative dance years had coincided with the disco craze, she heard the first beats of a waltz with serious trepidation, but she slid her right hand into his raised left one, and set her fingertips on his shoulder. She could feel his hand span her waist, and she moved closer, letting instinct guide her to a perfect place within his arms. In another moment he began to move her gracefully around the floor. Either he was an incredibly smooth dancer, or she was standing on his shoes.

She closed her eyes and let herself imagine that he pulled her nearer to feel her hair against his chin. On the next turn, he loosened his arms again, and she looked up to see him smiling.

"We're neighbors," he said.

"What?" she asked.

"You live in Harmony, Minnesota, right? I live in Blue Gill."

She was so startled, she lost her rhythm for the first time, then quickly recovered. She'd assumed he lived in Montana or perhaps back east. But by Minnesota standards, he was practically in her own backyard.

"That's only two hours away," she said.

"Right," he said.

She saw him watching for her reaction, and the too-polite angle of his eyebrows made her suspicious.

"What else do you know about me?" she asked.

"Well, I've had only a couple of hours to investigate." He steered her adroitly past another dancing couple.

"That should be enough to cover my whole life," she said.

He laughed. "Not quite. Just the important things."

"Such as?"

"You're single."

Well, okay, she thought.

"Did they tell you if I have a boyfriend?" she asked.

He shook his head. "If he was important, he would be here with you."

That just about summed up her feelings exactly. Still she winced over an uncomfortable recollection.

"What else did they tell you?"

She thought she could guess. She was the same age as Briana—twenty-six. She worked for a canoe outfitters company that served the major park areas in northern Minnesota. Her parents had been invited to the wedding, too, but lived in Dublin, Ireland, and couldn't attend. No one else there except Briana knew the more complicated details of her love life, and she doubted Mr. Inspector would have grilled the bride.

"They said you're independent as a moose," he said. "But smarter."

She gave a brief laugh. "Who did you talk to?"

"I promised not to tell."

Then Josh guided her around the floor with more fluid sweeps, and she realized before he had just been letting her get comfortable with the rhythm of the waltz. She tried not to concentrate too hard, letting herself trust the music and the sure, steady arms of the man who effortlessly spun her with him through the other dancers, until the lights and colors beyond his shoulder blurred into a heady collage.

When he finally slowed, she could feel the pleasure radiating from her face and could see the answering enjoyment in his dark eyes.

"You've danced before," she said.

"A little." He grinned.

His modesty was too much.

"I never asked about you. Are you single?"

For an instant he looked almost displeased, as if it irked him that she hadn't checked up on him. The waltz came to an end, and Amy drew out of his arms, turning to face the musicians and clap, noticing how the mirror ball reflected light into even the far corners of the room.

She glanced up at him. "I'll take brooding silence as a yes."

"I'm sorry," he said. "I thought I'd answered."

"Does that happen very often? You forget to talk?"

"Only when I'm thinking."

"I never realized thinking and talking were mutually exclusive."

He smiled, his eyes narrowing slightly at the corners. "You'd be surprised."

The musicians started playing a disco number, and Amy mentally cringed.

"It's a little warm," she said. "Shall we try the terrace?"

She slid her hand onto his arm and walked with him out to where the terrace was bathed in evening light. She looked up at the first stars nearly drowned out by the full moon; she couldn't believe she had to leave this beautiful place in just a few more hours. Amy reached into her satchel for her watch and held it up in the dim light to read the dial—7:02.

"What kind of watch is that?" he asked.

She registered his surprise and quickly hid the watch back in her satchel. It was a man's diving watch, one she had bought on sale because it was waterproof and durable. It was far too black and chunky to wear

with her dress, but she didn't like being without it, and
so she'd found a use for her satchel.

"It's just a watch," she said. Her fingers circled
within the soft fabric and she frowned, pulling out his
handkerchief. "I still have your handkerchief."

He shook his head, and when he leaned one hip
against the terrace railing, the angle of his jacket
showed the cool white of his shirt and the trim lines of
his cummerbund and trousers. Behind them, the music
and candlelight drifted softly through the French doors.

"I can see you haven't spent one instant thinking
about me," he said.

She smiled and offered the handkerchief. "Here."

"You keep it."

She felt an instant of confusion, then reluctantly slid
it back in the satchel. "You sure?"

"Since you wouldn't take the moccasins, at least accept the handkerchief," he said. "How'd the shoes turn
out, anyway?"

"Don't start this again. I'm not taking them off."

He laughed. "I just hope I didn't step on them too
much when we were dancing."

"You know you didn't."

She turned to face the water, leaning against the
railing. Moonlight sent a silver gleam along the water,
and she could see the hulking shape of the mountains as
they cut a high, ragged horizon against the sky. It was
so different from the horizons she knew back home, but
breathtakingly beautiful, and she couldn't help feeling
the magic of the night.

"Briana timed the wedding for the full moon," she
said softly.

"Where were you on the last full moon?" he asked.

Amy liked the question. She had to think. "At

home. I noticed it when I was coming in with the groceries." Without wanting to, she remembered listening to Andy's message on the answering machine that night as well, but she quickly dismissed the memory.

"You buy groceries at night?" he asked.

"Is that so strange? That's when I have time. Where were you on the last full moon?"

He shifted so that he was also facing the lake, and she looked over to see his profile. She had a feeling he had something to tell her, something he would say only if she waited.

"I was at my ex-wife's funeral," he said quietly. "I saw the moon that night from the front step of her house, when the last guests left."

It took her an instant to put together all the information: Josh had been married once. He'd divorced. And now, just recently, his ex-wife had died. It was an enormous history. She couldn't begin to imagine what he was feeling. How different the whole wedding today must have been for him, while for her it had been full of merriment and sweet yearning.

"Do you have children?" she asked, her voice soft and low.

In the moonlight she saw him turn his head to look at her, and his eyes were inscrutable. She had no idea what he was thinking, or why he looked at her that way, but she felt her heart ache for him.

"I have two girls," he said. "Chloe's eight, and Hannah is six."

"And they live with you?"

He nodded. "I just got them back a month ago, when their mother died. My parents are with them while I'm here for the wedding."

"Wow," she said slowly.

His low rumble was only partly a laugh. "Wow is right."

And then Amy did something she'd never done before. She knew it was wrong. She knew it went against every code of behavior she'd ever known. But her instincts told her that he was lonely, and that this must be a difficult time for him. Without knowing any of the details, she knew he suffered, and grieved. Her heart was full of the generous romance and hopefulness of the wedding, while her body was still warm with the memory of their waltz. She put her hand on his where it rested on the railing, and when he turned toward her, she slid near to him and lifted her face. With her lips parted slightly, she gazed up at him, trying to see into his dark eyes.

She heard him groan, then he closed his eyes.

"You're a devil sent to torture me, aren't you?" When he opened his eyes again, they gleamed with a raw, self-mocking quality.

She felt an exquisite ache of longing go through her, and caught her breath. She stayed where she was one instant longer, willing him to respond, then realized she was insane. Her gaze faltered.

"Don't go," he whispered, and pulled her slowly into his strong arms.

His gray eyes seemed to devour her, and she remembered again the determined strength with which he'd canoed across the lake. Josh Kita might be controlled and graceful with a waltz, but he restrained a savage power that lurked behind his hooded expression. The realization excited her, sending a shiver of expectation down her back.

What the hell am I doing? Josh thought, holding his desire fiercely in check. With her gypsy eyes and her chin a little too pointy, she was as lovely and luminous as the moonlight reflecting upon her impossible hair. And he was . . . Josh didn't know what he was anymore, but he knew this was wrong. He couldn't kiss her, not the way he wanted to, when they hardly knew each other, when it was the moonlight talking and he was old enough to know better.

She began to smile that sideways smile that made it hard for him to remember he was a gentleman.

"Who are you protecting?" she asked.

"You're not supposed to read my mind," he said.

"Then stop me."

Every muscle in his body tensed at the latent seduction in her voice. She couldn't have any idea how powerful an effect she was having on him. But damn if he could resist much longer.

Keeping one arm around her, he lifted her chin to tilt her face into the moonlight, vowing he'd give himself something to dream of, one good look before he returned to sanity and let her go. The slow curve of her too-wide mouth exactly matched the sweet, expectant smile in her eyes.

Oh, God, he'd already gone too far. If he'd ever had control of the situation at all, he no longer did.

As soon as she saw him leaning his face near, Amy closed her eyes and lifted her head, feeling the first touch of his kiss like a searing force that undid all other forces in her life, gravity included. She stood on tiptoe, letting her arms reach around his neck of their own accord. He was squeezing her tight against him and swaying so that she clung to him, feeling the heat of his body through the thin fabric of her dress. His lips were warm and yielding, then demanding and hungry, sweeping her into sensory overload. He smelled of the wedding somehow, excitement and spice, and when at last he lifted his mouth from hers, she gasped at the emotions that raced in her chest.

He lowered her so that she was fully back on the ground.

She opened her eyes and concentrated hard on his bow tie, fighting a wave of shyness that threatened the happiness she was feeling. She smoothed her hands down the front of his tux, resting them on his chest while he kept his arms around her. Her mind raced, but she was utterly speechless. She didn't know what she wanted him to say, but she prayed it would be soon.

Abruptly, he released her. Amy was so surprised she had to reach for the railing to keep her balance, and her gaze shot to his. He was looking toward the ballroom, where a group of people were standing in the doorway and seeming to stare at them.

Amy felt her cheeks grow warm with color, and turned toward the lake. She sensed Josh standing stiffly beside her.

"It seems to me we have a couple of choices," he said.

She didn't like the tone of his voice. It was too tight, too remote.

"What are they?" she asked.

"We could go back into the ballroom and pretend nothing's happened."

Ha! Fat chance. "Or?"

"We could go up to my room and finish what we've started."

He spoke with a hard edge that was unlike anything she'd known about him so far. Hurt and puzzled, she searched his expression. It was almost as if he was trying to be cruel, trying to reduce their kiss to a sordid exchange that would end as sex between virtual strangers.

She backed up a step, clutching her hands into fists. Her heart was sick with disappointment.

"I don't know what I expected," she said, "but it wasn't this."

For one more instant, he seemed frozen and aloof, then he came forward. "Amy, I'm sorry—"

"Don't," she said. "What were you doing? Can you honestly think I'd—" But then she remembered she'd initiated the contact between them, practically thrown herself into his arms. Her cheeks burned with humiliation. "Oh, God."

"Of course I know you're not—" He stopped.

An excruciating silence stretched between them, convincing her no one had ever felt more stupid or embarrassed. She stared blindly at the lake, and then the worst happened. Josh began to chuckle. She was so stunned, it took her an instant to realize the rumbling noise could be interpreted only as amusement.

"What on earth's so funny?" she demanded.

"I'm sorry," he said quickly. "I never meant to—"

"I have to go," she said, stepping away from him. She couldn't bear it anymore. The whole magical evening had been ruined. First he thought she was some cheap flirt, bent on seducing him. And then he had the gall to laugh at her.

"Wait a second."

"I have to catch my plane," she said, and backed away another step.

"You're flying out tonight?" he asked.

"Good-bye."

North Star Rising

She left him on the terrace. You should know better by now, Aim, she chastised herself, her heart pinched by bitterness and humiliation. Stupid, stupid Amy. She didn't even feel the pain in her feet as she raced up the long stairway, practically running to her room.

TWO

Josh turned up the music for the girls in the backseat and tried to concentrate on the unfamiliar road. He'd been feeling like a jerk for the past two weeks, and it made him irritable and bad with directions. He never should have kissed Amy. That was obvious. And then, he laughed when she was mad. He was a total jerk, he thought. He used to pride himself on being a basically considerate guy.

"Not around Amy," he mumbled.

"We can't hear our music," Chloe called. "Turn it up."

"I just did." But Josh turned it up another notch anyway.

Though he'd been busy juggling deadlines and the kids, he'd thought a lot about Amy in the weeks since the wedding, knowing he owed her a decent apology, feeling the weight of procrastination as he delayed getting in touch with her. Why had he invited her up to his room? If he'd listened to his instincts at all, he'd have known she wouldn't be interested in a one-night stand. It was worse than that. He'd done it deliberately to hurt her. To stop things before they started. To be absolutely sure she wouldn't think about him after the wedding, or try to start some long-distance relationship. Her trusting, upturned face and bewitching mouth resurfaced in his memory without warning, and he frowned grimly at the road. It didn't matter that one kiss had left him effectively brain-dead, all circuits beyond meltdown. He wasn't interested in any relationship, long-distance or short. It was best she knew that about him.

So then, what was he doing going to see her? A prick of excitement tried to penetrate his consciousness, but he crushed it down. Damn the woman. A decent apology. That was it. Nothing more. Then he could get on with his life with a clear conscience. He tried to picture her in the office of a canoeing outfitters, and took another look at his map.

"There it is! There it is!" Chloe yelled from the backseat.

He saw the sign: a bright blue billboard of a wild river and a red canoe shooting rapids between dangerous-looking boulders. The copy read: HOME TRAIL OUTFITTERS 5 MILES. IS YOUR LIFE JACKET FASTENED? The next four billboards had equally sensational pictures and more questions to get prospective canoers in the mood. Josh recognized effective advertising when he saw it, and guessed considerable capital must be backing Amy's company. When they reached the last curve and slowed into a parking lot, Chloe and Hannah were practically jumping out of their seat belts in their eagerness to look around.

From the parking lot, they could see that the Labyrinth River widened into a long, narrow lake, and that a

cascading stream entered from the right under a pretty
arching bridge. Picnic areas were visible across the lake
and behind the office, and wooden signs pointed toward
trailheads. Every inch of the scene was inviting and natural, from the cool, reflecting surface of the lake, to a
bright clutch of daffodils in the dense shade of a pine.

"We aren't staying, remember?" Josh warned them.
"I just have to talk to somebody here a minute. Why
don't you go look at the bridge? But don't leave my
sight."

The girls, in the leggings and sweaters they'd worn
to ice skating lessons, held hands and walked sedately
toward the bridge, surprising him with the maturity and
self-control they always demonstrated in public. He still
wasn't used to all the different ways they could behave
in a span of five minutes, but he knew his ex-wife had
been very strict with them about manners and respect,
and they were fairly predictable around strangers. With
a pang, he remembered how they used to accord him
the same politeness, relegating him to stranger status
until they became reacquainted with him on custodial
visits.

Josh slid his keys into his pocket and started toward
the office. With each step he felt increasingly uneasy,
even anxious, and at the same time he felt an almost
physical need to see Amy. Would there be any of the
intense chemistry he'd felt between them before, or had
that been merely a by-product of the wedding and the
moonlight? This would be a lot easier if the chemistry
was nil.

He took a quick look toward the bridge. His daughters were still there, now waving long stems of grass at
the water. Then he let his gaze wander over the dock
area. It was a busy place, he decided. Farther down the

shore, a couple of men were working on a rope of buoys and weights. He could hear the whine of a saw from a barn behind the office, and when he glimpsed the outlines of several canoes and kayaks, he assumed it was a repair shop. Another outbuilding had two tables with umbrellas before it, while a menu board printed in bright blue lettering advertised chili as the house special. The sign on top read DINAH'S DEPOT. The office was attached to a long, low building with spacious windows, and even from outside he could see it was packed with every kind of gear a canoer could want to rent or buy. Though the place wasn't packed, there were at least a dozen cars in the lot, and Josh assumed there were parties out on the river. For an afternoon in early June, it wasn't bad.

You're stalling, he warned himself, feeling a rise of anxiety in his gut.

He paused on the doorstep of the office and watched as an elderly couple stepped out of a canoe onto the dock. They reached back for their paddles and hats and a cooler, while one of the staff people, knee-deep in the water, steadied the canoe for them. Josh watched the couple laughing as they walked toward him, and when he looked back at the canoe he was surprised to see that the staff person had somehow flipped the canoe up into the air and was carrying it overhead, by a shoulder yolk, toward a rack.

That guy's got some strength, Josh thought.

The staff person angled the canoe gently on the rack, and then came out from underneath, her blond braid flashing forward over her life jacket.

Josh felt his blood drain into his shoes. Amy?

His gaze was irresistibly drawn to her as he tried to reconcile his memory of a girl in salmon-colored chiffon with the strong, agile woman walking toward him. She slipped off her life jacket, and though it was a cool afternoon, she wore only a tank top that revealed strong, tanned arms and square shoulders. Her breasts were full and firm under the white cotton of her top, with the outline of a lacy bra faintly visible through the fabric. The shirt was tucked into her shorts, where a worn leather belt accentuated her narrow waist. Her khaki shorts had cuffs that set off her toned legs, and the feet that he'd last seen in high heels were now in gray wool socks and hiking boots. The hiking boots, he noticed, were wet. She'd worn them right into and out of the lake.

Life jacket in hand, Amy looked ahead to the office and found Josh Kita standing on the front step.

Oh. My. God. The life jacket slipped from her grasp and fell to the dirt. She leaned quickly to recover it.

She'd been up since five-thirty that morning, and for the last two hours she'd been teaching couples from the local senior citizens' home how to paddle like old-time voyageurs and picnic like modern omnivores. It was work she loved, a program she'd designed herself, but she didn't need to look down at herself to know what gear she was wearing and how it must look to Josh.

Not that she should care, she thought, feeling the slow burn spread across her cheeks. He should be blushing, not her. *Come up to my room.* She remembered his biting words with quiet anger. She peered at him sharply, judging that his face could use a little color, and she refused to acknowledge that, despite his pallor and his lack of tuxedo, he was still devastatingly attractive.

"Excuse me," she said, and opened the door nearly in his face. "I need to get some coupons."

She retreated into the office and reached across the counter for the coupons and a catalogue. What was he doing there? She tried to calm the ragged beating in her chest. He was actually *there*.

She glanced out the window and saw him strolling toward the bridge, his hands in his pockets, his gait relaxed and comfortable. The sunlight fell on his dark hair and the shoulders of his brown sweater, and she instantly resented how at-home he looked. Larry, the accountant, was talking to Rex in the back room, and they both peeked out to see if she was a customer needing assistance. Amy gestured with the coupons before she headed back out.

It took her only a moment to say her good-byes to Maude and Hart Lovelace. Then there was no choice but to follow Josh to the bridge and find out why he'd come. She took a deep breath to steady her nerves. Why did he have this effect on her? He was like a math test. Or a trip to the dentist. Or the top of a roller coaster.

She slung her braid behind her shoulder and started toward the bridge. Two girls were playing with wisps of grass, dangling their legs through the railings. One of the girls had loose shoelaces, and despite herself, Amy smiled at the inviting picture they made. Under the big pine at the base of the bridge, beside a bench, Josh stood with his gaze directed toward the girls, his profile toward Amy, but she was certain he knew she was approaching.

She slowed her pace and tried not to feel self-conscious when Josh finally turned to meet her. His gray eyes regarded her with warm intensity, as if they were friends who should be glad to see each other. Not in a million years, she thought.

"Your daughters?" she asked.

He nodded. "We were here for skating lessons at the Nadja Rink."

She knew the rink; it wasn't far from Labyrinth Lake. "Isn't that a long way to come for skating lessons?" She stopped a couple of paces away and lifted her voice slightly over the cheery splashing of the stream.

He ran a hand through his hair. "I have a small seaplane, and I dock up at a resort in town," he said. "But I'd drive the two hours anyway. Skating's one of the things they love to do, and I thought it would help the transition better if they could have some continuity."

Amy smiled, secretly impressed by his casual mention of owning a plane. Not every dedicated father had the means to indulge his daughters so thoughtfully. "That's pretty nice for them."

He laughed slightly. "Not really. I used to think parents were crazy about the things they'd do for their kids. Now here I am doing the same thing, and it's no big deal."

He sounded both surprised and pleased with himself, and despite her determination to remain politely uninterested in him, Amy wondered what the story was with him and his children. Hadn't he shared custody with his ex-wife? How long had they been divorced?

"Has the skating helped the transition?" she asked.

Josh squinted slightly as he looked at his daughters. "Hard to say. I think they enjoy it."

She felt a tug of sympathy for the unspoken struggle

behind his words, and wasn't sure what to say. He glanced back at the parking lot as another car drove in.

"You're probably busy," he said.

"I am." Maybe he'd get to the point of his visit so she could get back to work.

"This looks like a nice business. How long have you worked here?"

"On and off since high school," she said. "I was a guide during summers in college. This year I'm back to oversee the expansion. It's kind of a boom or bust year for the owner, Rex."

He looked over as another car pulled into the lot. "It seems to be thriving."

Amy took the observation as a personal compliment and smiled. She didn't let herself think about what would happen if this summer wasn't a success for Rex. "We're booked through the rest of the month. We'll see what happens."

She glanced beyond him to watch his girls, who were coming down the bridge and heading toward the swings. She felt increasingly awkward, still not sure why he was there.

"I didn't realize you were a guide yourself," he said.

By the way his gaze landed on her shoulders, she guessed he was thinking about how she'd carried the canoe. It was mostly a matter of practice and balance, but she could see him looking at her arms as if weight-lifter's muscles might suddenly pop out.

"Why, is there something wrong with that?"

"No-o," he said slowly.

She laughed. "No-o," she mimicked. "One of our other guides is a woman too. Wouldn't you like your daughters to think they could grow up and be wilderness guides someday, if they wanted to?"

He answered without hesitation. "Of course."

"Well, there you go."

"You said you were here to oversee the expansion, though," he said.

Amy smiled, pointing a finger at him. "That's true. I lead trips only when I get the chance. Otherwise, I handle the advertising, design new programs, put out our catalogue, and brainstorm for more ways to expand. Rex handles the hiring and day-to-day operations. Larry does the accounting, and Rex's daughter, Dinah, runs the food service. It's almost like a family."

Josh's eyebrows lifted in continued surprise. "What's your business background?"

Why do you care? she thought, increasingly impatient to know why he'd come.

"I don't have an MBA, if that's what you're asking," she said. "I majored in economics, and I seem to have a knack for expanding things." She thought of all the work she'd done for her brother, Sean, and his wife, Cottie, when they started their photo and video business, and how that had led to other consulting positions, but Josh couldn't want to know about all that. Sean had begged her to stay in the business and become a partner, but Amy could never be fully happy with work that wasn't connected to the wilderness of the northern trails.

For a moment she considered telling him about the French Canadian voyageurs of her ancestry and the love of nature that she'd inherited from her father. But he'd asked about her business background, not the real background that mattered.

"It's a boring story, really," she finished.

Josh nodded slowly, as if he agreed with her that it

was boring. He confused her. He absolutely, totally confused her.

The reason she'd liked Josh Kita was because not once during the whole wedding had he ever looked at her like a buddy. He'd seemed interested and innately respectful and full of fascinating, magnetic energy. She thought he'd seen her as a whole woman, smart and desirable and vitally alive. That was, until the royal insult. That had proved he'd seen her as only a body. Then he'd gawked when she lifted the canoe. Now, seeing him gaze down at her as she stood beside him, she noticed a considering, thoughtful look in his eyes, and she knew it was happening. Category: Woman with Brain and Business Savvy. Beware. She was sick of being categorized.

Enough, she thought.

She picked up a stone and pitched it hard into the river. "I'm going to have to get back," she said.

"Wait. I've got something for you." He pulled a black diving watch from his pocket and held it toward her. "Is this yours?"

Her gaze flew from the watch to his eyes, and she smiled as she reached for it.

"I found it on the terrace, after we—after you left," he said. "I thought maybe it was yours."

"*That's* where I left it." She fastened the thick black band around her slender wrist. She had to brace the band against her waist while she fit the catch through the first hole so it would ride up on her forearm. "I looked all over for it," she said. "It's my favorite watch. I thought I'd lost it in my hotel room. It must have fallen out when I took out your handkerchief."

The excitement and heady happiness and fury of that night flooded back into her memory, making it impossible for her to look up at him. It was strange to think he'd been keeping her watch for her all this time, and yet he hadn't called. Now that it was back around her wrist it seemed to grow unusually warm, as if his fingers were grasping her instead.

Inside, she still burned from the last time he'd touched her. "I threw out your handkerchief," she confessed.

When he struck a fist against his chest, she glanced up at him.

"Ouch," he said with a wicked, sideways grin.

Don't pull that on me, she thought, but she knew his charm was already eroding her resistance.

"I want to clear up something," he said, his tone serious again.

"Is this why you came?"

"Yes."

She saw him glance back to the play area, to where his daughters were still happily pumping on the swings. By turning slightly, he began walking along the path of the little stream, and she joined him as it looped under shady pines back toward the playground. The serenity of the setting seemed to accent the awkwardness between them.

"I'm sorry for what happened at Lake Eloise," he said. "I should never have suggested you come up to my room. It was inappropriate and disrespectful, and I'm sorry."

Amy didn't want to remember how their kiss had ended. For two weeks she'd been trying to ignore the pain, with only her pride to comfort her, and despite her bravado and throwing away his stupid handkerchief, it hadn't been easy. Now his apology reminded her just how much she'd wanted to believe in the magic of their one kiss.

"It was nothing," she said. "Forget it."

He shook his head as if he wasn't satisfied. "I didn't want you to get the impression I was interested . . ." He paused. "Interested in anything lasting. That's why I said it."

She lifted her eyebrows and looked up at him. "Excuse me? Am I to understand you weren't interested at all, or you were interested only in something temporary? Which is the correct insult?"

She saw the ruddy color come through his complexion, and his eyes narrowed slightly. She stopped and put her hands on her hips so he was forced to turn and face her.

"You're so exasperating," she said, finally giving vent to all her frustration. "First you kiss me, then you insult me, then you show up unannounced to return my watch and . . . and . . . *linger*. Then you insult me again. What are you, interested in me or not?"

He put up his fist and coughed into his hand.

"Well?" she demanded.

Josh gave a disarming laugh. "All right. Okay. I was. I mean, when I met you at Lake Eloise, I definitely was. That's how this mess started." His warm grin made her suspicious.

" 'Mess'?" she echoed.

"The timing's all wrong. My ex-wife has just died, my kids are crazy. You live two hours away, and you must be ten years younger than I am. I'm being ridiculous just for thinking about it. But this week I found I couldn't forget you. What's that supposed to mean?" His voice dropped to a low, inviting rumble. "You tell me."

Amy felt herself soften considerably under the effect of his sexy voice. Not to mention his honesty. The age thing hadn't even occurred to her. "Just how old are you?"

"Thirty-six."

It was actually a ten-year difference. She slowly relaxed her arms and linked her fingers behind her back. "Halfway to seventy-two," she said pensively. Then her gaze shot to his.

Josh was wincing, but then he responded to her teasing expression by gritting his teeth. "You're different than you were at Lake Eloise."

"Yeah," she said. "The bridesmaid dress doesn't really go with the boots. It's a tough choice."

Josh laughed. "You made quite a Juliet, though."

Amy kept her smile up but felt a twinge of disappointment. She *had* felt magical and romantic on that balcony, but that side of her didn't fit in her everyday life. The hard part was, she really was both women, but the clothes showed only one side at a time.

"You'll just have to look me up again the next time I'm in a wedding."

"A wedding where all the bridesmaids carry canoes," he said.

Amy laughed, a mirthful, musical sound that carried through the trees to the swing set. Both girls looked up.

Josh swore and pulled Amy with him a couple of steps until they were concealed behind a thick spruce. Her pulse took off at an alarming rate.

"Laugh like that again and I'll have to kiss you," he warned her.

She shook her head, smiling at him. The pungent pine needles looked deceptively soft behind his head, while his eyes were focused on her with sharp intent.

When she felt his warm, strong hands cradle both of her bare elbows, ribbons of pleasure laced along her nerves. Patterns of light and shade dazzled over his brown sweater, and she had to squint up at him.

"You'd kiss me even in these boots?" she asked.

"Especially in those boots."

"If I let you kiss me, then you'll only insult me again."

"I won't," he said, leaning close.

She saw the individual black eyelashes rimming his mesmerizing eyes, and felt as vulnerable as a hypnotized bunny.

"Will," she whispered.

"Won't," he said, and kissed her. He just tipped his face near until she had no choice but to close her eyes and tilt her mouth upward and let her lips meet his. Their bodies barely brushed each other, and his kiss was the merest whisper of pressure on hers, but she felt liquid heat roll thickly inside her, rendering her breathless. She leaned closer, increasing the pressure of her lips on his, and she heard him mutter a low groan as he stepped back.

He quickly released her, folding his arms across his chest. She could see his eyes darken with unspoken emotion, and her fingers tingled to reach out for his face, knowing it would be warm to the touch.

"So now what?" she asked. Her voice was almost unrecognizable to herself, it was so low and smoky. She smiled with soft shyness. He did this to her. He changed her whole body, even her voice, with just a kiss.

His heavy-lidded eyes flashed with dark humor. "Know any insults?"

Amy let out another peal of laughter, and this time

Josh's two daughters deserted the swings and came around the spruce to find them. There were a dozen things she wanted to say to him, but the girls were pulling on their father's hands, saying they were thirsty.

"I want you to meet a friend of mine," Josh said to his daughters. "This is Amy Larkspur. You know the wedding I went to a couple of weeks ago? She was one of the bridesmaids. This is Chloe." He put his hand on the taller girl's head, then gestured to the younger girl. "And this is Hannah."

"It's nice to meet you," Amy said, smiling. "How was skating?"

"Bad," Chloe said.

Amy liked her honesty, though the answer surprised her.

Chloe's expressive eyes were enlarged by a pair of glasses, and her thin brown hair fell straight to her shoulders. Her face was fuller than her little sister's, and she had pronounced cheekbones that offset the glasses and gave her an angular but attractive look.

"Chloe thinks her teacher smells," Hannah said.

"I didn't say that," Chloe said.

"It's her perfume," Hannah said. "What's a musk?"

Amy laughed. Hannah's wavy blond hair was tied back in a ponytail, her narrow nose matched her slender face, and her blue eyes had an exotic charm to them. Amy glanced up at their father and recognized the slightly Asian shape, if not the color. His wife must have been very fair, she guessed. His children were arresting in an unusual, interesting way.

"I couldn't tell you what musk is, offhand," Amy said. "Did I hear you were thirsty? We have Popsicles, if that's okay with your dad. My treat."

Josh agreed, so the girls ran toward Dinah's Depot while he and Amy followed.

"You have beautiful children," she said.

"Thank you."

"Is *Kita* a Japanese name?"

"Yes. My great-grandparents came to Blue Gill from Japan. The name means 'north.'"

She thought it must have been unusual for a Japanese family to come to an area settled primarily by Scandinavian immigrants, but felt shy about prying further and he didn't volunteer any more. As they walked back, she checked the lake and saw one of the other guides out with a class of beginners, teaching them to flutter their paddles. She reached up for her shoulder and gingerly squeezed a sore muscle. Josh's gaze followed the movement.

"Who takes care of you?" he asked softly.

The question came out of nowhere and utterly surprised her. "What?"

"The girls and I have each other now," he said. "What about you?"

Amy turned to face him, wondering at the quiet speculation in his eyes. He seemed to be asking an absolute, fundamental question, as if he were asking how she breathed. She didn't know how to reply. Her mother and stepfather lived abroad. Nearby she had a brother and a sister-in-law whom she loved dearly. But she knew that wasn't what Josh was asking about. She could have had a husband by now, maybe even kids of her own, but Andy had been wrong for her, and she didn't regret the choices she'd made.

"You don't need to rub it in," she said, trying to keep her voice light.

"It's your shoulders that look like they could use a rub."

Her heart made a queer sideways leap. "You wouldn't be volunteering, would you?"

He buried his hands in his pockets, and when his eyebrows lowered in an enigmatic frown, she felt the sunlight in the space between them begin to shimmer with subtle sexual tension. It made her feel taller and oddly expectant, as if even now invisible fingers were reaching to massage her shoulders.

"Kind of sounded like it, didn't it?" he said. He seemed to have decided something. "Have dinner with me."

She smiled and curled a loose hair back around her ear. "Now, why would I go out with an older guy with two kids who says he isn't interested in a relationship?"

His eyes were unwavering. "You have no choice," he said. "How about Monday? I could pick you up around six."

"Who'll watch your daughters?"

"My parents. They live around the corner from us in Blue Gill, and they babysit part of the time when I'm working."

"That's convenient." She hedged. Somehow the idea of having dinner with him was like an invitation to go skydiving. "What do you do for a living?"

"I'm a computer game designer," he said, and lifted one eyebrow in anticipation of her reaction.

Amy couldn't help being surprised. He seemed too normal. Well, not normal exactly, but he didn't seem nerdy enough to be a computer type. And she hardly knew anything about computers. She could feel a gulf opening up between them. But what had she expected;

that he was a lawyer or a businessman or a real estate agent?

"How interesting," she said.

But he laughed, as if he'd guessed her real thoughts. "I know. It's a geek thing. I love my work, though, and it's turned out very well for me. I specialize in games for girls. It's risky, and creative, and I can work in the middle of the night. It suits me. Really. And I'm not a total nerd."

His voice had turned sardonic at the end, and she looked up at him, trying to read the unintended meaning behind his expression. He sounded as if he'd met skepticism about his work before, and she had a feeling her own reaction meant a lot to him.

She gazed out at the lake, and a flash memory of him paddling across Lake Eloise surfaced in her mind. If she wasn't the feminine bridesmaid he'd first thought she was, then he wasn't exactly what she'd thought he was, either.

She glanced back toward Dinah's Depot, where Chloe and Hannah were intently licking their Popsicles: red and yellow.

"I don't know much about computers," she said. Or daughters. Or men wealthy enough to own seaplanes.

Even though she wasn't looking at him directly, she sensed his disappointment. It was in the way he didn't make a lighthearted joke. It was in the way he took his hand out of his pocket and brushed it through his hair, as if remembering something or somebody else.

"Six o'clock Monday," he whispered in her ear, and then he walked on to join his daughters.

Harmony, a small, unpretentious town on Birch Lake, was southeast of International Falls and a twenty-minute flight north of his home in Blue Gill. Glaciers had covered the area four times before the last one receded permanently, and the grinding had scooped out a huge area behind the town, leaving an arched hillside that sloped down to the wide, deep lake. Josh knew the terrain from his previous flights, but that Monday evening clouds obscured his view, and he landed on the lake and motored to the dock at the resort shortly before the rain began to fall.

He'd bought a station wagon to use in Harmony when he flew the girls up for skating lessons, and as he unlocked it in the resort parking lot, the solid vehicle struck him more as a family car than it ever had before. Or maybe the car was reproaching him for being there without the girls.

No. This is a good thing, he told himself.

Half an hour later, he peered out the rain-streaked windshield and checked the number on the mailbox. Amy's home was a small two-bedroom saltbox with wide-screen porches on the southern and eastern sides, and it clung to the hillside overlooking Harmony like one of the gnarly, windswept pines that surrounded it.

Every window was dark, as if the little house were trying to sleep through the dismal rain, and Josh recognized the obvious: She wasn't home. Yet, he hoped. It *was* Monday. He doubted she'd forgotten their date, and she didn't seem like the type to be late. Maybe her electricity was out.

The idea made him smile. That woman had more electricity in her than a thousand lightbulbs flashing in synch. Why else would he be there? He waited another five minutes, and then his impatience and the monotony of his wipers got the best of him. Anything would be better than waiting in the car.

By the time a pickup truck pulled up before the house, the rain was coming down in torrents, and Josh had lost any last shred of romantic pleasure from standing under the dripping front awning of her house. He watched her pull a bag of gear out of her car, slam the door, and dash through the rain toward the door. She was practically all the way to the house before she saw him, and then she squeezed herself beside him onto the dry top step.

"What are you doing here?" she asked, speaking loudly over the noise of the rain.

Excellent. He opened the screen door for her and they moved under the cover of the porch roof. "We had a date," he answered with matching volume.

She checked her watch. "But I left you three messages. Have you been here since six?"

"I was early," he said.

Framed by her damp hair, her eyes rounded with guilt, and then he was subjected to a once-over that did nothing for his pride. She almost seemed to enjoy how wet his black leather shoes were.

"I'm really sorry," she said. "I tried to reach you. I have another commitment tonight that I completely forgot about until yesterday. It's been on my calendar for weeks, and I just didn't put it together."

"I'm glad you're amused. What's the other commitment?"

Instead of answering, she looked him over again more slowly. He hoped she realized exactly what she was blowing off. Beneath his jacket he wore a crisp blue shirt with a jazzy tie and black pleated trousers. He'd even gotten the girls' input on whether he looked nice or boring, and he'd believed them when they said he was the handsomest daddy on the planet. Now he felt absurd. When she noticed that he was hiding one hand, he reached forward, holding a single calla lily, white and superbly curved in the misty dimness.

"Oh, Josh," she said. "It's beautiful."

As she reached for the delicate blossom, a car door slammed loudly from the street, and he saw her start with alarm.

"Oh my God. Come in." She quickly opened the door for Josh to enter.

Josh looked over his shoulder toward the street, but she urged him into the house, turning on some of the lights to beat back the damp atmosphere of the rain. She dumped her gear at the bottom of the stairs and gave him a quick smile.

"Try to act natural," she said.

"What's going on?"

"I'll go put this in water." With the calla lily, she started for the kitchen to find a vase. "Don't stare at the turban."

Turban? It had been bad enough waiting for Amy in the rain, thinking she'd forgotten their date after all, or worse, she was in a car wreck. Now she had another commitment. He couldn't wait to see the other guy.

THREE

The doorbell rang, and since Amy was still in the kitchen, Josh reached to open the door. A trio of women stood on the porch, and if he felt surprised, the three of them looked utterly dumbstruck.

The lady in the blue turban spoke first. "Who the devil are you?"

"I'm Amy's jilted date," Josh answered solemnly.

"Oh my gosh," said the youngest woman, a petite redhead with a winning smile and a conspicuously pregnant figure. She pushed forward and held out her hand. "I'm Cottie Larkspur, Amy's sister-in-law. It's about time she had a date, but I swear, she could have at least warned us to bring more chicken." Cottie walked past him into the house, carrying a paper bag of fragrant take-out chicken. "Amy?"

The third woman half hid behind her bag of take-out. "I'm Olivia," said a tall, dark-haired woman in her late forties with shy eyes. "Pleased to meet you. I didn't catch your name?"

"Josh Kita," he said, reaching for her bag of food and shaking her warm hand.

"Are you related to the Kitas in St. Paul? The iron people?" the woman in the turban demanded. She was a generation or two older than Amy, with extra rouge and false eyelashes that seemed coordinated with the butterfly decals on her pantsuit. If pressed, he would guess she spent a lot of time at bake sales and fundraisers.

"The Kitas in St. Paul are my uncle's family," he answered.

"Then you must be David Kita's son," she said, moving into the living room. "I'm Madge LaFarge, and I knew your dad in high school. We used to take tours of your grandparents' mine, years ago, after the war. They moved out of iron before all the taconite business, didn't they?"

"Yes, ma'am." He felt his ears grow red while Madge proceeded to tell him his own family history, complete with the expansion of the iron mine that had made his family's fortune, three generations earlier. She rattled off half a dozen other families in the iron and lumber industries, families that were the backbone of various arts and philanthropic organizations to this day, names integral to Minnesota's history. She obviously took an interest in the history of the region, dwelling on the glories of development rather than on the complex effects that had followed the ravaging of the state's natural resources. In addition, she had all the more personal information that everyone in his parents' generation seemed to know about the Kita family, including his first marriage.

"Didn't you marry a girl from California?" Madge asked.

Josh glanced over at Amy, who was setting the table

in the dining area, and he had the feeling she was listening even though she didn't look up. He noticed she'd taken a moment to change into a blue skirt, and the full material fell softly from her slim waist.

"I did. But my wife and I divorced five years ago."

"Did you ever play bridge with her?"

Josh gave a slow, sideways grin. "Can't say I did."

Madge nodded wisely and exchanged looks with Cottie and Olivia. "How about Scrabble?" she asked him.

"We didn't play Scrabble, either."

"Well," said Madge. "That explains it. How are those paper plates coming, Amy?"

"All set," Amy said.

She and Cottie had set paper plates and a bottle of wine on the dining-room table, then spread out the take-out containers with a feast of chicken, mashed potatoes, corn muffins, gravy, and peas, enough to feed the five of them and leave leftovers. If Amy thought he was going to take a hint and leave, she was going to be sorely mistaken, he thought. Nothing could make him pass up a night with Amy and the three Furies.

He pulled up a chair next to Amy, who passed him the chicken, and then began one of the strangest evenings he'd had in a long time.

Madge, Cottie, and Olivia were as different from one another as they were from Amy, but they shared a genuine camaraderie. They ate like truck drivers, then dumped the paper plates and plasticware in the garbage and unrolled a green felt cloth on the table. Like a bridge queen in her turban, Madge was Amy's partner, and she played effortlessly, making dry jokes and outrageous comments while she ate chocolate-covered nuts. Cottie, who sat on Amy's right and clearly adored her with sisterly love, tended to laugh at her own mistakes and apologize as she laid her cards. Olivia played with vicious concentration and wouldn't speak unless she was bidding.

Josh had never played bridge before, having always suspected it was a dull game, but as he sat beside Amy, letting her teach him the rudiments of counting face-cards and aces, bidding, and trying to take tricks, he grew interested in following her thought processes. Maybe he could try a bridge paradigm for a cooperation game, he thought, remembering a computer game design that had been stumping him.

Once, when Amy was the dummy, she went into the kitchen to start water for tea, and when they dealt the next hand, he picked up her cards to put them in order for her. When she came back, she leaned over his shoulder and inspected the cards.

"Go for it," she whispered.

So he played the hand in her place, checking with her when he was in doubt about what to play, and he and Madge won the rubber with a small slam.

"Not bad, young man," Madge said. "Not bad at all."

"I like games." To put it mildly. It occurred to him that none of Amy's friends had grilled him about what he did, as if they didn't use jobs and status as a way to judge or categorize people. They seemed to accept him as Amy's friend, unconditionally, and the experience was novel to him. Watching Amy thoughtfully, he tried to figure out how her friends reflected qualities in her own personality.

Cottie pushed back from the table and patted both hands on her rounded belly. "I know when I'm beat."

Olivia pushed her chair back too. "Nice playing," she said. "Next month at my house, all right?"

"You aren't going!" Amy protested. "I just started the tea water."

Madge collected the cards into a pile. "I like to end on a small slam."

Josh watched as Amy encouraged her friends to stay for another rubber, but they all seemed to need to get home, and in another few minutes, they were heading out the door.

"Give an old lady your arm," Madge said to Josh.

Madge looked about as fragile as a bulldozer, but he knew a command when he heard one, so he escorted her out to the car.

"You learn pretty quick," Madge said.

"I never paid any attention to bridge," he said. "It has a lot of possibilities."

"*Lots* of possibilities," Madge said, with a sly expression.

Olivia and Cottie laughed, opening their car doors. Madge sat heavily in the front seat and braced her be-ringed hand on the interior handle of her door, poised to close it. "If you want to play bridge with Amy, you take my advice and don't let her push you away like she does all the others. She has enough 'friendly guy friends,' if you know what I mean."

Josh wasn't sure he did. "What advice will you give Amy?"

"Same as I always give her. It's a happy salmon that can swim upriver."

Josh laughed, and when Madge gave it a tug, he closed the car door for her. She was a daffy old dragon, that was for damn sure. He'd have to remember to tell his parents he'd run into her.

Their car circled the cul-de-sac and headed down the road, taillights glowing red at the corner. Josh looked up at the dark, starless sky, and noticed that while the rain had stopped, the air was rich with moisture. He turned and walked slowly back toward the house, marveling that he felt so at home with Amy's friends after such a short acquaintance. Shannon's friends had always made him feel so awkward, so extraneous. So male. But then, Amy wasn't anything like Shannon.

Why did he compare them at all? he wondered, looking up at the house as he approached. He felt different now that the others were gone, sort of wary and expectant, as if this were a trick-or-treat house he was approaching for the first time. But it was an utterly adult sensation. He squared his shoulders, sliding his hands in his pockets.

Amy was standing in the doorway, holding a candle in a hurricane globe. She smiled that sweet, too-wide smile he liked as she set the candle on a low stool in the corner of the screened porch. Her blue skirt followed the contours of her hips and knees, and her legs were bare above her worn loafers. An elastic band clasped her curly blond hair in a low, loose ponytail that kept her forehead and throat exposed. The soft light illuminated a porch swing and the fanning leaves of a potted palm, and Josh closed the screen door carefully behind him, hearing the latch click.

"Thanks for staying," she said. "I'll just get a sweater. Will you be warm enough?"

"I'm fine."

Fine enough to eat for dessert, Amy thought, turning quickly to stop herself from staring at him. Again. She slipped back inside and reached into the closet for her warm cashmere cardigan, the rose-colored one her mother had sent for her birthday. She'd been staring at him all night, completely unable to keep her eyes off his subtly changing expressions. As she pulled the soft sweater around her, she shivered again, and realized she was more nervous than cold. He was way too incredible. So try not to fall all over yourself, idiot. Clearly he was willing to stick around for a while.

She stopped in the kitchen for a couple of teacups and the pot, gripping it hard with a hot pad on her way back to the porch. The bridge group had left fast enough, with that none-too-subtle exit. Amy would bet a thousand dollars Madge had said something embarrassing out by the car. She bit inward on her lip, peeking through the screen door to where Josh stood by the porch swing. What was he really doing there? The truth still shocked her: He had *stayed* for *bridge*. How many guys would do that?

With an elbow she nudged the door open, and Josh looked over. In one long stride, he was there to hold the door for her.

"Thanks," she said.

"I hope that's hot enough," he said. "Your cheeks are nearly blue."

"I'm just nervous. I mean, just cold," she corrected herself. Then she laughed. "I mean, I'll be fine."

Josh smiled and sat beside her on the wide, old-fashioned porch swing, which was angled so they had a view of the town and lake off to the side of the house. Most of the expanse was a deep, purply black, but there were dots of yellow and white from buildings in the town, and a spot of red out across the lake. A slight breeze lifted upward toward them, carrying the heavy scent of the wet earth and leaves.

Amy nestled the hot teacup in her hands and felt the warmth seep into her cold fingers. Breathing in the fragrant aroma of the tea, she made an effort to relax the tension in her shoulders, but just sitting near Josh was having a curious effect on her, kind of like stomach cramps, but nice.

"How long have you been playing bridge?" he asked.

"Oh, for about three years. Cottie got me into this group, actually. Madge is her neighbor, and Cottie became friends with Olivia when she approved a loan for her at the bank. They needed a fourth, and Cottie thought I needed some women friends."

Josh smiled. "Was she right?"

"I guess," Amy said. "I had friends at the university, but none of them live up here, and with my mother in Ireland, Cottie and my brother, Sean, are my only relatives nearby. The bridge group keeps me connected. How about you? You must have friends." From what Madge had said earlier, his family was one of the most wellconnected in Minnesota.

"My friends are all on the Internet," he said. "We E-mail each other and meet up at the toy conventions."

Despite trying, she couldn't picture him in front of a computer screen all day. He seemed too active, somehow. With a glance at his trim thighs outlined by his black trousers, she had the impression his body was larger than before, almost crowding her own body as they shared the porch swing.

"I don't have much time for friends otherwise," he added, "especially now that I've got the girls back."

"They're with your parents tonight?"

He nodded. "My parents would love to have them

every night, if they could. They're trying to catch up too."

Amy took another sip of her tea, then used the toe of her loafer to push the swing backward an inch. She felt the swing adjust as Josh shifted his weight, then they began to swing slightly, with a tiny creak way up in one of the chains; he was helping to push.

"Tell me about your girls," she said. "How old were they when you divorced?"

"Three and one." He laughed softly. "You know those beanbag animals that are so popular right now? My kids have a dozen of them, and they were playing beanbag funeral when I left."

Her eyebrows lifted in surprise. "Isn't that a little dark?"

"It's better than nightmares. They're both afraid to sleep alone these days. Sometimes I don't know. Chloe's having the hardest time with it."

"How did your wife die?"

"My ex-wife," he corrected. "She was stopped at a red light one night, coming home from the library, and a drunk teenager took a wild right turn and plowed his pickup right into her. Shannon was dead instantly."

Amy felt a shiver and pulled her sweater more closely around her. "I'm so sorry."

She could see Josh's chiseled features by the dim candlelight, and his face was serious, his brows furrowed. "Nobody deserves to die like that." His low voice was edged with anger. "My kids lost their mother because some idiot sold alcohol to an underage teenager."

She winced at his bitter tone. She was at a loss for how to reply, yet his emotion kindled a deep memory of a similar reaction. She knew from her own experience that death didn't care about being fair. She waited in silence, watching as he dropped his head and gazed down at his teacup.

"It's the strangest thing. Shannon and I tolerated each other, barely, for the kids' sake. We had an ugly divorce, and I didn't try especially hard to be nice or fair to her. I'm not proud of it," he said. "But when she was killed, I had this heavy, weighing guilt about it. It was as if the whole accident was somehow my fault. And now I can't help feeling so incredibly glad to have my daughters back in my life."

Amy felt a twist of compassion. She had loved her father so dearly and dreaded his death for so long, and yet when it happened, there had been an end to the strain and suffering, an end to the constant watchfulness. Her grief had been mixed with relief, and she had felt guilty about it for ages. "You don't have to be ashamed," she said.

"That's what it is," he said slowly. "You've put your finger on it. I'm ashamed that Shannon's dead, because now I've got the girls."

Amy breathed in slowly as she tried to puzzle out what it must be like for him. He must have had deep feelings for Shannon once, and even though they'd divorced, her death must be a strange thing to deal with.

"It sounds like you have a lot of contradicting emotions," she said finally. "It has to be hard to claim them all at the same time."

He lifted his face again and laughed briefly, his gaze toward the dark lake in the distance.. "I want to hear about you. Tell me about these men in your life that Madge referred to."

Amy groaned, her cheeks growing warm. "Now there's a nonsequitor," she said, but she could respect that he wanted to change the topic. She set down her cup and leaned back more comfortably in the swing, slipping off her loafers, drawing her knees up and letting Josh take care of keeping the motion going. "Don't tell me Madge said something about the friendly guys."

"Those are the ones," he said, turning his head to smile at her.

Amy gave an exaggerated sigh. "She thinks she knows everything about my love life, but she doesn't. She's the consummate matchmaker. She hooked up Cottie and Sean, and she's been working on me and Olivia. Olivia's fine with it. All she knows is the bank and she's so shy she'd never meet anyone without Madge's interference. But all the men Madge sets me up with are, well, I don't know."

She couldn't believe she was discussing this with him.

"They're what?" he asked. "Too boring? Too lazy?"

"No," she said slowly. "They're usually smart, and hard workers."

"They have no charisma? No sense of humor?"

She laughed. "Oh, no. A couple of them were real cards. One guy painted his motorcycle pink to make me laugh." He'd also thought it was funny to run red lights, she remembered.

Josh tipped his face slightly, watching her. "Then what? They had no sex appeal?"

Amy slanted her eyes sideways. "Ah . . ." she began. She thought of Brad. And then Andy. And then all the other guys who had tried to get beyond kissing her good night. Her cheeks slowly grew hotter. "You don't want to get into this," she said.

"Oh, yes. I do."

"Not really."

"Yes, really," he said.

"Well, what about you? You've been divorced five years. Haven't there been any other women in the picture?"

"Ha!" He gave a laugh, and the swing went wide on an extra hard push. "Shannon was enough to last a lifetime, believe me."

"But not anybody?" she pressed him. "Not once in all that time?"

She didn't think she'd believe him if he said there'd been nobody. He was simply too handsome. When he didn't answer immediately, she shifted uncomfortably and realized that if he told her about his women, then out of fairness she'd have to tell him about Andy. It had been over a month since Andy's last phone call, but she still cringed mentally when she remembered how he'd called just to let her know he was doing fine, really fine, so fine that she could listen right past his actual words to the loneliness behind. She hoped Josh didn't have a similar lost lover in his recent past.

"Well?" she said. "I think you forgot to answer again."

"This is the question of women in my picture, correct?"

"Correct."

She could see him studying her, as if deciding whether to tell the truth.

"I don't think a couple of one-nighters count for much," he said carefully. "And I realized pretty fast that sex for its own sake doesn't satisfy me for very long. There are risks too. It isn't worth it."

Amy nodded, pulling her ponytail forward over one shoulder. She found his answer was more intimate than she'd bargained for, and she judged from the way he casually shifted his legs to cross one over the other that he was not uneffected by their conversation, either.

"I'm sorry we didn't get our date," she said.

"At least you didn't totally stand me up."

"I thought you'd get my messages. I really did call you three times. Don't you check your machine?"

"I would have ignored the messages anyway," he said.

With a prickling of expectation, she watched him, waiting for more.

"I don't take excuses very well."

"But what if I hadn't come home at all?"

He hunched a shoulder. "You did."

Just barely. She frowned as she remembered her drive home in the rain. She'd been so furious that she'd been in more danger from her own preoccupation than from the rain, and it had taken great effort to force herself to drive safely.

"What is it?" he asked.

She shook her head. "Work. I had a fight with Larry."

"Is he one of your friendly guys?"

At first she didn't know what he meant, then she gave a short laugh. "No. He's the accountant for Home Trail Outfitters. He doesn't like what I'm spending on advertising, but Rex approved my budget and I'm right on target. Larry said I wasn't bringing in enough business to cover my expenses, but I'm sure I've brought in even more than I originally projected. When I asked to see the books, he was mortally offended. 'Be my guest,' he said. 'Why take me at my word?' So then I couldn't, and Rex got offended, too." She could picture the whole difficult scene all over again. "Larry's accusation doesn't make sense to me. I keep a head count of people coming through, and I know it's a fifty percent increase over last year. Those people generate a lot of revenue."

"What's your boss think? Rex, right?"

"Rex is committed to expanding, for his daughter Dinah's sake as much as his own," Amy said. "But I could see he was worried about what Larry said." She frowned down at her hands. "I don't know. This isn't the time to scale back, and I know that's what Larry would like."

She wished she knew more about Josh's business. He'd said something once about it being risky, and she wondered if he'd ever sweated over situations like hers before. It didn't seem likely, but she could certainly use some advice.

"Don't worry about it," he said. "Larry's just a numbers man. It's his job to be stingy."

"I don't know," she repeated. "There's a lot at stake." Like Rex's whole future, and Dinah's. And her own, to a degree. She unfolded her long legs and slipped her loafers back on, too anxious about her work to sit still any longer. "Do you want to see something?"

"Sure."

She switched on a floodlight that illuminated the dark, wet grass, and led Josh off the porch and down the sloping side yard to a low, small barn that had once stored gardening equipment and drying racks for the previous owner. She stepped in ahead of him to pull the cord of a bare overhead lightbulb, and the light revealed an assortment of storage things—skis, a lawn mower, a garbage can, a couple of paint cans, a bicycle, an old umbrella. But the main space of the barn was taken up by a long, gleaming canoe that rested upside-down on a pair of saw horses along one wall. With an old sorrow weighing on her heart, she touched the satiny, golden wood, gently trailing her fingers down the arching belly of the canoe as she preceded Josh farther into the shed.

She was afraid to look over at him, afraid to let him see what it meant to her to have him there with her.

"Isn't it lovely?" she asked. "My father made it for me."

She didn't realize that her husky, quiet voice revealed a strange hint of longing, and that Josh wasn't fooled by the way she shielded her eyes from him.

"Your father?"

"Mm-hmm," she murmured. "He made it for me for my sixteenth birthday. I used to tell him when I grew up I wanted to spend every night in a different place, camping and canoeing forever, free and wild. So he made me a hope canoe. Like a hope chest, only a canoe. He wanted me to have it for when I got married someday."

She heard the stiff creak of the wood as he leaned one shoulder against the doorjamb.

"He was thinking ahead, I take it," Josh said.

She nodded. "He had cancer. He knew he was dying. He wanted to give me something that would last."

"Oh, Amy," Josh said softly.

She leaned her head back and blinked at the misty halo around the bare lightbulb. She tried to laugh. "Talk about contradicting emotions."

"What was he like?"

"He was a park ranger," she said. "He taught me everything. I could steer a canoe before I could ride a bike. He knew about the trees and the loons and the stars. He took us on canoe trips where there weren't any trails yet, and he could spot a ripe blueberry from a hundred yards away."

"He sounds wonderful," he said.

Sean had been away at college during the last autumn, and she'd been in high school, trying to keep her grades up and study for her driver's license—all while helping her mother with her father's medications and trips to the doctor. There had been mundane chores to do side-by-side with her father's inspiring dignity. She'd seen her mother try to hide her own suffering, seen the two of them napping on the couch together. As the leaves turned colors and the weather cooled, she had watched his decline, praying it would somehow turn around. And then had followed the mute anguish of his last few hours when he forgot who he was, forgot he was dying, and wandered into the laundry room, looking for his compass.

Amy slowly traced the bottom seam of the canoe and willed herself to be strong. Her dad might not be there to walk her down the aisle someday, but he'd left her this canoe. A loop of her hair slid forward on her cheek, half shielding her from Josh, and she could feel his unspoken empathy in the silence. Earlier that night she had wanted to extend her compassion to him, let him know that she accepted even his less admirable responses to Shannon's death. Now she could feel his steady support as surely as if he'd put his hand on hers.

"He was a modern day voyageur," she said. "There was nobody ever like him."

When she looked over, his eyes were shadowed with concern, and his low voice resonated quietly in the narrow space. "I'm sorry, Amy."

But she didn't want to feel the loneliness that hovered at the edge of her consciousness.

"He died ten years ago this summer. When I got back from Lee and Briana's wedding, I made myself a promise. I told myself that if everything worked out for the Home Trail Outfitters this summer, I would take out my hope canoe for a maiden voyage. As a reward."

He didn't smile. "Your dad wanted you to have it when you got married."

"My dad wouldn't want me to leave it here waiting unused anymore," she said. "It's such a beautiful canoe."

"You wouldn't dare take it out."

She didn't know why his certainty troubled her so much. "Yes, I would."

"Come here, you," he said gruffly, and moved forward.

At first she couldn't respond, but when he grasped her cold fingers in his and gave a tug, she turned and stepped into his embrace, closing her eyes as his strong arms circled around her.

"Weddings are awful," Amy said against his shoulder. "I thought I was crying because I was happy for Briana, but it's really terrible to watch your best friend get married. You feel so left behind."

Josh held her closer and laughed gently. "I could have told you that."

"Does that make me selfish and mean?" she asked.

"You're asking the guy whose children play funeral games with their beanbag animals, thanks to his deceased ex-wife."

She looked up at him. "And you're not too twisted, are you?"

He laughed again. "Not too."

When he ran his thumb along the curve of her cheek, she liked the way she felt against him, the way he made her feel light and heavy at the same time, delicate boned and strong.

"You shouldn't take out your hope canoe," he said. "Even after the outfitters is a success this summer. You should save it."

For marriage? For true love? They were nice ideas, but she had long since abandoned her misty girlhood dreams. A good canoe was something she could appreciate. Marriages like her brother and Cottie's or Briana and Lee's were too rare to make her believe in her own chances.

"What do you still believe in?" she asked.

His gaze was steady and thoughtful, his head very near. She thought he would recognize the hypocrisy of him telling her to save her hope canoe when he had seen his own marriage end in divorce. She thought she would see the cynicism, the hard edge that had made him shatter the magic of their first kiss by Lake Eloise. Instead he turned her slightly, so her back was to the canoe, and she could just feel the wood behind her waist.

"I believe in the present," he said. "I believe in my children."

She searched his eyes and knew he spoke the absolute truth. While she admired his convictions, deep inside she envied him too. It wasn't fair. He had children; people to love.

"Don't think so hard, gypsy," he murmured.

"I'm not—"

His lips were against hers, as warm and seductive as they had been in her dreams. She tipped her face up and leaned against him, instantly aware of the sweet electricity of his hard body against her own. It was as if her skin could feel all the way through her clothing to the heat of his chest, and still want more.

His kiss grew more insistent, molding her lips to

his, while she felt his hands span her waist and travel up her back, drawing her even more tightly against him. She locked her knees in an effort to keep her balance, but a bone-melting desire was stealing through her, and she realized with relief that Josh had settled her between the smooth wood of the canoe at her back and his own, solid body. She half swooned at the pressure of his legs against hers, effectively pinning her upright, and she linked her arms around his shoulders, extending her belly and breasts upward against his torso.

He moaned, and she felt his kiss move to the base of her throat, where his touch caused a molten ecstasy of response. She twined her fingers in his thick hair, inhaling the clean, damp scent that lingered around him, as if he were part of the rain and the night. As his mouth moved lower down her neck, she arched back against the canoe, and when he brought his hand around her to run his palm slowly under one breast, she felt a heady rush of desire.

A clutch of miniature explosives detonated in her gut, driving a spiral of desire outward through her body. She moaned and tucked her head to kiss the warm skin under his jaw, while trailing her fingers down his back, letting her fingernails pull at the weave of his shirt. He made her feel liquid and blind and expectant all at the same time.

The canoe shifted slightly behind her, and he straightened.

"You okay?" he murmured.

She opened her eyes and blinked, focusing on the shadowy features of his handsome face. She lifted her thumb and set a kiss on it, then gently traced her thumb over his lips.

He let out a low groan, then smiled sideways at her.

His eyes gleamed with lazy sexuality, and she felt him massage her back warmly as he held her near to him.

"Something gives me the feeling we've been here before," he said.

"You don't mean the shed."

"I don't mean the shed." He brushed his lips lightly over her eyebrow, then her cheek, then hovered near her mouth.

Amy felt the new softness in her lips as she smiled up at him. There was no wedding in the background to distract them, no children waiting nearby. If she wanted to, she could invite him back into her house and they could explore each other intimately as long as they liked. The idea made her close her eyes with the promise of desire, then his lips touched hers again, causing her to respond mindlessly, deliciously.

Yet even as her passion was at the brink of sliding beyond her control, a faint warning came from the recesses of her mind. By Josh's own admission, he was capable of having a one-nighter with a woman, but Amy knew she would never be happy in that sort of situation. He'd also made it clear that he wasn't interested in a long-term relationship, though he hadn't repeated that lately. What did that leave?

As if sensing her hesitation, he paused, his mouth lifting to hover a mere inch from hers. She tried to read his expression, but the light was behind him and his eyes were hooded and dark. A smile lingered in the angle of his elegant lips, and overall he looked as if he . . . As if he was waiting.

"Can I ask something?" she asked quietly.

His eyes narrowed, and he dipped his head near for another light kiss. "Sure."

"What are you expecting from me?"

His eyebrows rose a fraction and his arms loosened, but he didn't let her go. "You mean, beyond tonight?"

She had an uneasy feeling he'd just answered her question. She backed away sideways, and Josh finally let her go. When she reached the doorway, he was still standing beside the canoe, frowning.

"What is it?"

Amy shook her head and tried to order her racing emotions: regret, desire, fear of angering him. "I don't want to mislead you," she said. "I'm attracted to you. Really attracted. But I don't casually sleep with anybody."

"I didn't think you did," he said.

"Then—" She gestured toward the area where she'd just stood.

"It was a kiss, Amy. Just a kiss. Or two."

"Or three."

"Or three," he acknowledged. "Maybe a little hotter than we could have predicted, but that's all it was."

"That's all?"

"Am I missing something?"

How could he look so cool about it? She'd felt more excited in two minutes in his arms than she'd felt during a whole night of making love with Andy. She didn't even want to begin a comparison between Josh and Brad. In her experience, sex was about getting emotionally hurt, or hurting someone, and she didn't know which was worse. And there was no way a kiss like his was just an idle gesture. It had "prebedroom" written all over it.

"I guess we have different definitions of 'just a kiss,' " she said, hoping she didn't sound as vulnerable as she felt. She put her hand on the doorway and turned, then stepped out quickly across the damp grass.

"Amy!"

When she didn't stop, he swore under his breath, and then the shed door slammed. Her heart leaped, propelling her forward, but he was behind her in a second, and he gripped her hand so tightly she had to pivot toward him to keep her balance.

"Lord," he said. "What have I done to make you think you have to run away from me?"

"Let go of me," she said, twisting her fingers free.

"Listen to me," he said forcefully. "I don't know what your experience has been with other men, but there is no reason to bail on me. It was only a kiss, Amy, not some plot to get you in bed. I am your basic, decent guy."

"No, I already slept with my basic, decent guy. His name was Andy, and you're nothing like him."

Josh looked surprised, then determined. "Come here." He was frowning, but his voice sounded like he wanted to laugh.

Amy backed up another step.

"The thing is," she said, "I *want* to sleep with you. I get vertigo just standing close to you. But responsible adults—"

"Come here," he said again, and this time when he stepped near and pulled her into his arms, she clung to him fiercely, fusing her mouth to his with all the pent-up frustration that had haunted her ever since she'd first seen him in that damn canoe on Lake Eloise. It was no use pretending she didn't want him. Every inch of her body craved him, and he'd have to be an idiot if he couldn't tell.

❖━━━━━━━❖

Josh could tell all right. It was nearly killing him. It had occurred to him in the shed that there was nothing to stop them from continuing their intimacy in the privacy of Amy's home; or right there in the shed, for that matter. He hadn't started out with a plot, but he'd been receptive when the possibility occurred to him. Now she was expecting him to have willpower for both of them, and damned if he knew how he was going to come up with it. She was the hottest creature he'd ever met, all fire and melting passion, and it took only the slightest contact with her feminine, seductive curves for him to feel the heat ignite between them. She was like candies in a jar—safe as long as the jar was on the shelf out of reach, but as soon as the first piece was unwrapped, he wanted to consume all the sweetness until there was nothing left. And he had one of those candies melting on his tongue at that very moment.

"Josh," she murmured.

He pressed her nearer to him, ignoring her plea. He could feel her response, knew the exact instant when she ceased resisting and unleashed the subtle, tantalizing sexuality that she kept in check, perhaps without even being aware that she did. He felt it in her hips, in the way she not only moved nearer, but swayed against him in an inviting, intimate dance. And her fingers, which before had brushed through his hair, now found the sensitive area behind one of his ears and traced a path down his jaw, scouting out a trail for her lips to follow. He could feel the swelling of her breasts against his rib cage, and he sucked in his belly, anticipating that she was about to touch his waist just above his belt buckle, and then she did.

"Oh God, Amy."

He'd never felt less decent in his life. All he wanted to do was guide her hand lower, to feel her fingers through his trousers against his arousal. He forced himself to wrap his arms tightly around her, pinning her in his embrace so that she'd have to stop. The floodlight from the house illuminated their area of the sideyard with a gray pragmatic light that dulled everything to an even hue. Josh focused on the wooden shingles of the house, shifting to ease the discomfort of his arousal. His movement caused Amy to stiffen, then she tipped her head back to look up at him. If he expected innocent surprise, what he found instead was the beguiling hint of a gypsy smile.

"I like being with you," she said.

"So I see."

"You make me feel—different."

He laughed briefly. "You make me feel a lot more than different."

She watched him with frank interest, then her eyes narrowed and she ran a mischievous hand up his tie, trailing the back of her finger over his Adam's apple. "Maybe I'm wrong about making love," she said. "Maybe it doesn't have to be such a serious thing, so fraught with unspoken expectations. Maybe it could be just fun. You're the game master; what do you think?"

She was going to drive him utterly mad, that was what he thought. He curled her hands forward until he could hold them in both of his own. Then he kissed her in a friendly way.

She frowned. "You're not patronizing me, are you?"

"No," he said. "I'm rescuing myself. You, Amy Larkspur, are too seductive for words. Way out of my league." He realized she had just articulated the sex-for-fun motto that had carried him through both of his one-nighters, but coming from her, it sounded both blasphemous and incredibly sexy.

"Oh, come on," she said.

"I mean it. I'd like to say I'm being chivalrous, but I'll tell you quite honestly it's my own sanity I'm concerned about."

She tipped her chin up, and a musical, heart-lifting laugh resonated around him. "Very funny, Josh."

"Funny would be trying to say 'sex for fun' and 'responsible adult' in the same sentence."

Amy looked quizzically at him, then twisted her lips. "Kind of inconsistent, isn't it?"

"Understatement of the evening."

She laughed again with delight. "I never got to be inconsistent with anyone before. Usually a woman gets hammered for that. It's kind of nice."

"Great," he said. "Glad you tried it out on me."

She pulled one of her hands free, tucked the other securely inside his palm, and walked with him, hand in hand, toward the front of the house. It was all he could do not to pivot her against him again, but it frightened him how much he wanted her. Not for her body alone, not for the way she'd moved against him as if she'd just awakened to her own sexuality; he wanted her laughter, her teasing, her frowns, and her pensiveness. He craved the elusive essence of Amy herself. And for more than one night. That's what frightened him and what finally compelled him to slow down.

Some first date this had turned out to be.

He didn't want to be her spontaneous experiment in sex for fun. The idea was a shock to him and revealed why her words had seemed blasphemous. For him, it could never be just sex with Amy. If they ever made love, it would be a whole lot more. He felt a tightening in his gut, a warning signal that suddenly made his body grow chill.

She's the one, he thought. *Whether I'm ready or not.*

FOUR

When Josh called the next morning to invite her to visit him for an afternoon in Blue Gill, she was relieved, pleased, and altogether nervous.

"You might want to double-check your calendar for another bridge conflict," he said dryly, and she laughed.

Several days later, Amy slowly pulled up the driveway, unrolling her window and turning off the radio so she could feel the sweet breeze on her cheeks and hear the gravel under her tires. The sunlight, landing hot on her dashboard as she turned the car toward the house, caused her to squint. Josh's place was set way back from the highway, with a wide, sloping meadow of unmowed grasses and wildflowers descending gradually to her left, and a view of the Blue Gill River valley. With a white facade, his sprawling home was a combination of log cabin and ranch styles that crossed an old-fashioned look with contemporary angles. She liked the huge white pine at the side of the house, and the two swings that hung on long ropes from one of the branches. As she stopped the car, she noticed two dips of dirt under the swings, worn down by the girls. Everything about the place, from the black mailbox to the copper-green weathervane on the apex of the roof, conveyed a sense of easy prosperity.

Amy, however, felt anything but relaxed. The whole two-hour drive she'd kept exceeding the speed limit accidentally, as if her own anticipation were driving the car. She was going to *Josh's* place, she kept thinking. The man who was inexorably wedging his way into her life with a calla lily and a hand of bridge and a kiss that defied all previous experiences. And now, for the first time, she was going to him.

Taking her keys, she shut the door of her pickup, straightened the back of her sundress, and walked through the afternoon heat toward the front door. She half expected her old dog Misty to come running around the corner of the house, and she smiled at the wind chime of pewter animals hanging from the awning. When she was just about to ring the bell, she saw the note taped to the door.

"Oh, no," she said, taking the yellow slip between her fingers. His handwriting was large though somewhat illegible.

Amy—
    I'm at [something something] up Chloe. I'll be back soon. Come in and [something] at home. [Something something] the mess.

                                                            J.

Trying the paper at different angles, she guessed he'd gone to school to pick up his daughter. If it weren't so hot in the sunshine of the front yard, she wouldn't have dreamed of going in, but the temptation of getting out of the heat was irresistible, so with a twinge of guilt, she allowed herself to be curious and pushed the door open.

"Wow," she whispered, as cool air enveloped her body.

Josh's home was beautiful, spacious, and different. Everything was blue, white, and a golden brown wooden color that made her think of watercolor paintings. By descending a couple of wide, brick stairs she reached a living room where the white walls rose clear up to the wood beam rafters, twenty feet above. The stone fireplace, bracketed by bookshelves, had a strange, sculptured clock instead of a mantel, and the intricate cogs and levers made an audible ticking. To her right, five tall windows let in streams of sunlight that touched on bits of brass and textured fabric.

Then, as she glanced down, she saw the carpet in front of the couch was covered with Lego pieces, beanbag animals, markers, stickers, scissors, and shards of paper. At least three projects had been left midstream, a danger zone for bare feet. She mentally winced.

A counter separated the living room from a kitchen area, and when she moved nearer, she let her eyes scan over the cereal boxes, peanut butter, newspapers, coffee filters, and orange rinds. A row of Cheerios had been arranged on the windowsill, but there were an equal number on the floor, half crushed. She sniffed delicately, then peered in the sink.

She rolled her eyes away. "Yuck."

She stood another moment by the counter, undecided. She had to admit Josh's house made her nervous. She hadn't expected a dirty kitchen or a messy living room. If she'd thought of it at all, she'd assumed he had a housekeeper, or that his daughters were naturally neat. But here it was, two in the afternoon, and there were still cereal bowls in the sink.

A perky, cheerful woman would roll up her sleeves and start cleaning. She'd have that kitchen scrubbed up in no time. She'd have lemonade briskly stirring by the time Josh came back.

Amy wanted to croak.

With a wry smile, she walked back toward the front windows and idly picked up a tiny pirate figurine. Considering he'd left the note on the door, she had to assume he didn't mind if she saw the disorder. Then again, was she supposed to be honored that they hadn't cleaned up?

It wasn't that Amy was superpicky about cleanliness. What bothered her was something more subtle, something she wouldn't have felt if the place had been tidy. His home was a thoroughly lived-in, hands-on type of place, proof that Josh had a full and complex life with his children, a history and a future. As she saw a series of framed children's drawings going up out of sight along the wall of the staircase, she felt like a trespasser. An invited trespasser, but a trespasser just the same, and not only into the house. She felt a shiver of premonition, and shook her shoulders to try to dispel it.

Just then she heard tires on the gravel driveway, and walked quickly outside to see Josh pulling up in front of the house.

"Hi!" he called, slamming his door. "I was afraid you'd beat me back. You found the place okay?"

She nodded. Just the sight of him was enough to make her bones smile, and for the first time since seeing his note, she was genuinely glad she'd come. He went around the car and held the door open for his daughter

Chloe, who got out slowly, dragging a backpack after her.

"Is everything okay?" Amy asked.

"We had a little mix-up at school," he said. "The second graders have been working on a musical all semester, and since Chloe just started attending, naturally she hasn't learned the music. While they rehearse this afternoon, Chloe's going to take the rest of the day off."

"Mr. Perotti made me stand out in the hall," Chloe said. "And I was *not* causing trouble."

Though Amy didn't want to doubt the girl, she suspected there were two sides to this story. Josh rubbed the top of her hair, ruffling it. The girl shoved her glasses up her nose and gave her father a seriously annoyed look.

"We talked about this," he said. "Everyone's trying their best."

"Yeah," Chloe said. "Can I swim?"

"Pick up the Legos first. Then you can change. Don't get in the water until Amy and I are out on the porch. All right?"

"Is she going to swim too?"

Amy was surprised by the sullen resentment in the child's expression, but Josh didn't react to it.

"Not this time," he said. "Go on. We'll be out there soon."

As Chloe preceded them into the house, Josh came up to Amy and gave her hand a warm, solid squeeze. Though she sensed a degree of tension in his features, his gaze was attentive, as if he were noticing everything about her sleeveless dress, her hair, and her delicate earrings.

"I'm glad you're here. Did you see my note?"

"Your handwriting's deplorable," she said.

"I know. Especially when I'm agitated."

He spoke with a confidence that made Amy think of a different kind of agitation, and she noticed the tension in his features had been replaced by something else.

Josh's gaze dropped to her lips. "There are certain times, for instance, when I'd never try to write anything."

"Certain times when you're agitated?"

"Mm-hmm." He used his thumb to gently brush a tendril of her hair from where it grazed her cheek. She smiled up at him, waiting expectantly. This was why she'd driven two hours.

"Like now?" she whispered.

He chuckled low in his throat. "Wouldn't you like to know?" He touched her chin lightly and drew back from her. "Come in with me. This won't be quite the afternoon I had planned, but what can you do?"

She was walking beside him when all at once a loud squawking and an echoing banging noise came from the side of the house, followed rapidly by a scream from inside.

Josh began to run into the house. "Turn off the dryer!" he yelled. "There's a bird in the vent, Chloe! Turn it off!"

The squawks and bangs got even more frantic. Instead of following Josh, Amy hurried around the side of the house, past a row of tall lilac bushes, toward the source of the noise. A ladder had been propped up against the house just where a vent cover had been rotated at an angle. Bits of white lint clung to the shingles, and the frantic, birdlike bangs were coming from inside. She was starting up the ladder when the noises stopped, and a pathetic crooning noise came from the vent instead.

A window rolled open in the wall to her right, and Chloe's head leaned out, her cheeks covered with tears, her glasses fogged.

"Did I kill the bird?"

"Oh, no," Amy said. "I can hear it in there. It's probably just a little scared."

"I didn't know!" Chloe said.

Josh appeared behind his daughter and quickly gave her a hug. "It's all right, Chloe. Honestly. I forgot to tell you."

"I just wanted to dry the towel!"

Amy heard a small, impatient noise come from the vent. Apparently whatever bird had gotten into the vent was more annoyed than injured. It sounded exactly like a prima donna scolding a conductor. Amy looked back at Josh, who was looking at her with a strange expression. As she waited he began to smile, and then had to look away.

He was going to laugh! She wanted to die. Instead he snorted, and smiled down at the little girl.

"Chloe, listen," he said, gently touching her cheek with his fingers. "Listen."

Chloe turned, and then stuck her head out the window. All three of them listened to the silence, and then the bird did it again, a bossy, indignant squawk. Chloe and Josh grinned at each other, and then all three of them laughed.

"The poor bird," Amy said.

"I tried all morning to get the thing out," Josh said. "I'm going to have to rip out half the vent to get to it."

"How did it get in?" Amy asked.

"You got me. But it doesn't want to leave."

Chloe laughed again and took off her glasses to dry them on the bottom of her shirt. "Can we leave it in until Grampa comes?"

"Do we have a choice?" Josh said, laughing. "Maybe he'll know how to get it out."

"I'm going to change," Chloe said, and bolted out of sight.

Amy glanced over at Josh and felt a sort of charmed pleasure as she realized where they were. She was halfway up a ladder, holding tight to the warm aluminum rungs, and Josh was to her right and slightly higher, leaning out a large window. The bird was reduced to mere shuffling noises and an occasional peep, while below, dozens of daylilies offered their orange blooms toward the sky.

"Don't get dizzy, Juliet," he said.

"I was thinking the same thing. Or a reverse Rapunzel."

"You read too many fairy tales."

She felt a lightness in her gut. "I don't read fairy tales at all," she said. "I'm a very practical person."

"Oh yeah? Then how do you explain the rose in your hair?"

"I don't have a—" She reached up and felt something soft lodged in her hair and carefully extricated it to take a look: It was just a few petals of a lilac blossom, pale purple and very fragrant. She must have brushed against the lilacs as she ran past.

Josh was grinning at her. "Is it a rose, or is it a rose?"

She looked up at him as she let the blossoms fall from her fingers. "If I say it's a rose, then I believe in fairy tales. But lilacs are good enough for me, any day."

He leaned out a little farther. "Come up another step," he urged softly.

She eyeballed the distance and realized she'd be in range for a kiss if he endangered himself and leaned out a little farther. "No."

"Come on," he said.

She wanted to. Heaven knew she did. His expression was pure rakish magnetism, reaching her heart and giving a mammoth tug. She liked how his eyes looked perceptive when he was amused, and lazy when he was turned on, and just now his eyes looked both perceptive and lazy, to devastating effect.

He gripped the window casing and put a knee up on the ledge.

"Watch what you're doing!"

He just laughed, easily maintaining his balance at the brink of a free fall.

"Oh, for goodness' sake," she said, and ducked her head to begin descending the ladder.

"Meet me on the porch," he said. "Chicken."

"You're the bonehead."

"And you're so ladylike too."

"You once called me a moose," she called from the base of the ladder.

He grinned out the window. "I said you were *smarter* than a moose."

"Oh, that's saying a lot. That about pinpoints me in the Mensa range."

Josh laughed, and the bird in the vent made another squawking noise, as if to scold them into silence.

Minutes later, Amy was lounging in a comfortable chair, sipping lemonade and keeping an eye on Chloe in the pool while Josh straightened up the kitchen.

Because of the shade of the porch, it was hardly hot

at all on this side of the house, and the sliding door to the kitchen was open wide to let the breeze in and let Josh's occasional comments come out. She liked the un-cluttered, practical decor of the porch: the cushioned recliners and low, iron tables. Through the screen, she had an easy view of the fenced pool and Chloe as she splashed and swam in the clear water.

It took him only a minute to throw a load in the dishwasher, and then he sat opposite her with his own glass of lemonade.

"Sorry about the mess," he said. "Between the bird and Mr. Perotti, it was low priority. Cheers."

Amy smiled and tipped her glass against his. "Cheers."

She watched his throat work as he drained half his lemonade in long swallows, and he made her thirsty, even when she had a tall glass of her own, slick with condensation. Get a grip, she thought, but she couldn't stifle the tingling that originated in the soles of her feet. Because of Chloe's presence, Amy knew she and Josh needed to maintain some distance, but instead of feeling more aloof from him, she was more aware of him than ever. She wanted to reach over and touch him, to set her damp fingers on the warm, tan skin of his fore-arm. She could almost taste the sweet lemonade on his lips when he set down his glass and licked the moisture back, and yet all she could do was sit demurely in her chair.

She dragged her gaze toward the pool.

"How long has Chloe been swimming?" she asked. "She's really good." The girl was hunched over at the side of the pool, and after a careful moment, she dove headfirst into the water.

"Since she was two," he said. "Both the girls have had lots of different lessons."

"Such as?"

He gave a shrug with one of his shoulders, a gesture she was beginning to recognize meant he was uncomfortable or disapproving.

"I liked the swimming and the ice skating," he said. "They also took ballet, gymnastics, and karate, and had music appreciation lessons and French tutorials. They were signed up for day camp this summer, but of course that won't happen now."

His last words resonated between them, and she knew he was referring to Shannon's death. He kept his tone so neutral, she couldn't tell if he approved of all the lessons or not. She had a hard time imagining it would be fun, constantly going off to different activities. When she was young, she valued doing things with her family.

"Do they miss all of that here in Blue Gill?" she asked.

Josh shook his head, watching her thoughtfully. "All they miss is their mom," he said quietly.

The contrast of busy activity to a mother's love made Amy realize once again the enormity of the girls' loss, and she felt guilty for mentally criticizing the choices Shannon had made.

"What was she like?" Amy asked, her voice low.

Josh should have been ready for the question, but he wasn't. He looked at her hand and watched as she carried the frosty glass to her lips. Her cheeks were slightly pink from the heat, and the skin of her bare shoulders was tanned and smooth. She was wearing a rose-colored, flower-patterned sundress that managed to set off her curves and waist even as it fit loosely. If she wore any makeup at all, he couldn't tell, but her lips were a healthy, natural red, and her brown eyes and long lashes gave depth to her pointy, attentive face. With Amy before him, alive and vibrant, it was difficult to summon a visual memory of Shannon, but when he let his gaze rest on the pool and zoned out briefly, the memories came back, accompanied by old disappointment, then acrid humor.

"Shannon was a redhead." She had a great body, too, but he didn't say that. "She was very spontaneous, funny, and extremely intelligent. A lot like Chloe, actually, personality wise."

"How did you meet her?"

He scratched the hair above his ear. "She had some capital to invest, and she was checking out the computer software company I was working for out in California. My boss asked me to take her out to dinner and fill her in, so I did. She was sharp, I'll give her that."

Shannon was more than sharp. While selecting a company to invest in, she was also handpicking a dozen of the hottest software designers in Silicon Valley, intending to lure them to work for her. The dinner was part of a plan Shannon had devised weeks before. And when Josh later invited her up for a nightcap, he unwittingly followed the plan too.

But something went wrong. Shannon fell in love. With Josh.

He glanced back at Amy, and saw her watching him curiously.

"You frown when you think about Shannon," she said.

He laughed, and made a conscious effort to relax the muscles in his shoulders. "Habit."

"Why did you decide to marry her?"

"She was exciting to be around," he said with a shrug. He shifted in his chair to prop one ankle up on his other knee. "She wanted to make her first million by the time she turned thirty, and I admired her ambition and drive. I knew, in theory, that there were personal costs to that kind of ambition, but I didn't know I'd be paying them."

Amy leaned her elbow on the table and propped her chin on her fist. "What happened?"

"It's hard to describe," he said. Actually, it wasn't that hard to describe, but it wasn't very pleasant. Shannon grew to know him only too well. Whenever he began to challenge her actions she would fight with him first, then get him into a bed. If he argued that she was traveling too often, getting too obsessed with growing her business, she'd cancel a couple of trips and make love to him until he was insane for her again, and as soon as she was secure that he wasn't going to argue anymore, she'd return to her go-get-'em pace. Then there he'd be, lonesome for her, keenly frustrated, and feeling manipulated.

"We had our problems," he said. "But every marriage does. When Shannon got pregnant, I figured the pace would slow down a little, but if anything, she began to work harder, even when she felt lousy. She made her first million just a week before Chloe was born, and five weeks later, she was in Hong Kong for another deal."

Amy didn't speak though her expression was thoughtful, even grave. He ran a hand through the hair over his forehead, trying to figure out how to explain how it had gone wrong.

"I didn't want to criticize her. I supported her working, but I adored our baby and I wanted to be with her as much as I could. When Shannon was home, the last thing she wanted to do was discuss our problems. Then when Hannah was born, and Chloe was two years old, Shannon was gone two weeks out of every three. I had two babies, a sixty-hour a week job, and an absent wife. After a while, I just couldn't do it all."

He tipped his lemonade glass to drain it, but all that was left was a slim ice cube. He chewed on that. The stupid irony of it all still made him sick, but he'd gotten this far. He might as well tell Amy the rest.

"What did you do?" she asked.

He took a long breath and looked out to see Chloe floating in the inner tube, her fingers trailing in the water, one foot making occasional splashes: a picture of contentment. A fierce, protective anger rose in him, and he knew he could never do anything to jeopardize her well-being. Not after what they'd been through already.

"I quit my job," he said. "I started working free-lance out of our home. That way I could stagger my hours and still be there with the kids half a day."

"What's so wrong with that?"

He let his gaze return to Amy, and some of the old anger and shame faded away again. Something about her made it not so hard to tell her things, things he hadn't wanted to talk about with anyone else.

"Shannon presented me to the judge as an unemployed, lazy, TV-watching underachiever who couldn't even fry an egg, let alone take care of two little girls. According to her, I was a gold-digging geek who would stoop to using his own daughters as leverage against his hard-working wife."

Amy looked shocked, but he laughed with remembered disgust. Nothing compared to the rage he'd felt when the judge awarded full custody to Shannon. To fight it, he would have had to bring his girls into court, and he knew how traumatic that would have been for them, especially Chloe. It was the judgment of Solomon all over again, but between two parents instead of two women claiming to be the mother. In the end he let them go with their mother instead of forcing them into a situation that could be emotionally destructive.

"I believe in our judicial system," he said at last. "I know the judge made the best decision he could, but I don't think it was the right decision."

And for five years, Josh had paid for it. He set down his glass with infinite control and peered out toward the shimmering brightness of the pool. None of this had anything to do with Amy. He didn't know why he was troubling her with it.

"Do you think Hannah and Chloe have been all right, despite the divorce?" she asked.

He didn't know whether to be grateful or angry that she wasn't letting it drop. It was both painful and strangely satisfying to go over it with her, as if he was finally getting a chance to tell his side of it, and reveal all the long-term grievances that hadn't had their day in court.

"That's the million-dollar question that nobody ever wants to answer," he said. "The girls didn't have a choice, did they? A few months after the divorce, Shannon and the girls moved to Boston, and half a year after that, they moved to Seattle. I couldn't see that they were ever coming back to California, so I moved back home to Minnesota. That way when I did get my custody time, at least they would always be with me in the same place, and they could get to know their grandparents."

The whole thing was absurdly ironic. He knew the

judge thought he was awarding the girls to a mother who was caring and fiscally responsible, as opposed to a bum of a dad. But in the end, it was Josh who had a far more stable lifestyle, and his "unemployed" freelance work had turned into an innovative business grossing profits large enough to rival Shannon's.

He glanced over at Amy. "Your glass is empty."

She tilted her head farther over on her fist. "So is yours," she said. "I like trying to guess what you're not telling me."

His eyebrows shot up. "That was as thorough a version as anyone's ever gotten."

She made a quick, open-palmed gesture with her hand. "But there's something missing. The glue. Something kept you and Shannon together through two babies, despite your differences. That's no inconsiderable amount of time."

"Sex."

Her expression remained absolutely motionless, and then her cheeks began to redden. "Excuse me?"

"Sex," he repeated.

"I thought that's what you said." She turned in her chair so he could only see her profile.

Brilliant, Kita. Why don't you just nail a sign on your forehead that says NEANDERTHAL? At the same time, he felt a stirring of desire that had nothing to do with his dead ex-wife and everything to do with the pink-cheeked woman sitting across from him. The other night she'd been so passionate and eager in his arms, so incredibly sensual. He would never make life decisions based on lust again, but that didn't mean he had to ignore the sensations she roused in him.

"I've learned since then," he said.

"Learned what, exactly?"

Before he could answer, Chloe climbed up the porch steps and through the screen door.

"Where's a towel?" she asked.

"You put it in the dryer, remember?" He smiled and tossed her a clean one he had behind him.

Chloe wrapped up in it, holding a fistful of the blue terry against her wet chin. "Thanks." Her shoes were next to the door, and she reached into one and pulled out her glasses, then slid them over her ears. "When's Hannah going to be home?"

"In about ten minutes," he said.

"If we get the bird out, can we keep it?" Chloe asked.

"Not likely. We'll see."

"We don't have any pets," Chloe said to Amy.

Amy laughed, enjoying Josh's haggard expression. "I once had a dog named Misty," she said. "I'm thinking of getting another puppy."

"What kind?" Chloe asked.

"I don't know. What kind do you like?"

Chloe began to talk about dogs, then cats, then horses. She seemed receptive to any animal, as long as it was a potential pet. When she clapped her hands at one point, demonstrating how she would call a puppy if it ran off, Amy was reminded of a clapping game she'd known as a girl.

"Do you know 'Say, Say, Oh, Playmate'?" Amy asked.

"What's that?"

"It's a game you play with your hands." Amy sang the opening tune and made clapping motions in the air. "You need a partner. Come on. I'll show you."

Chloe hung back, then looked at her dad. "I don't think so."

"Give it a try, Chloe," her father said.

Amy made the motions again, smiling to encourage her.

"I don't think so. I'm going to play Legos." Chloe moved sideways toward the kitchen.

"Chloe," Josh said.

"It's all right," Amy said.

Chloe frowned at both of them and disappeared into the house.

"I apologize," he said. "That was inexcusably rude."

Amy clasped her hands together between her knees and tried to shrug away the awkwardness. She didn't feel hurt, but she could tell Josh was embarrassed. "It's all right," she repeated. "It's just a game."

"Will you show me?" he said.

Amy gave him a skeptical look.

"No, really." He hitched his chair around the table so he could be closer, opposite to her, and held his hands out before him. "Then I can do it with the girls." They heard the sound of a car driving on the gravel out front, and he clapped once. "Come on. We don't have much time."

She looked at his handsome face, close enough to touch, with his amused expression already focused on her hands, and his lips parted. Their knees were almost touching. A rush of sweet desire coursed through her, disturbing her far more than Chloe's slight ever could, and she swallowed to steady her voice before she could sing. Then she raised her hands to meet his and began the clapping sequence.

"It repeats," she said. "Say, say, oh—one hand, clap, the other hand, clap, clap. Two hands. Front, back."

Every one of her senses was alert and receptive as she taught him the game she'd learned in grade school.

While the light pressure of his palms met hers with increasing regularity, the last trace of lemonade on her lips made the song taste tart. The clapping made a percussive, pleasing sound, and the dry breeze smelled like the Junes of her childhood, tickling her memory. But the sight of him, his closeness, was totally part of the present, and she longed for the game to end so his concentration would leave their hands and his gaze would come up to meet hers again.

In another minute, the game did end, and he did look up. Once again, the now familiar feeling of a small, personal bomb detonating in her gut robbed her of speech. He was the most incredible, attractive, desirable man she had ever met, and his face was alive with more bemused sensuality than she could endure. She might be the teacher of this particular game, but there was no doubt in her heart that he was the game master.

"You're going to kiss me," he said, his voice low. "You can't help it. But you don't have much time."

She rested her fingers on his knees and leaned toward his face, holding his gaze with each incremental advance. In the distance she heard a door slamming and voices advancing, but she shifted her gaze to his lips and lightly touched her tongue to her own. Four inches away, she stopped.

"You were saying?" she asked.

"Oh, God."

She saw an entire kiss flash in the wicked light of his eyes and could almost feel his arms crush around her and the porch disappear. Noise was distinctly audible from the kitchen. She saw his eyes close, and then he carefully backed his chair away so that his knees slid out from beneath her fingers. When he opened his eyes again, his expression was accusatory.

"You're going to regret this, Juliet."

A rush of hot pleasure ran through her. "Promise?"

Josh laughed, just as a couple in their mid-fifties came through the doorway.

"Well, hello! Who do we have here?" said the woman, beaming at Amy.

"Hi, Mom," Josh said. He smiled at Amy. "These are my parents, Kristen and David Kita. This is Amy Larkspur."

"Nice to meet you," Kristen said. "Josh told us he had a surprise for us. Aren't you lovely?"

As Amy shook hands with Josh's parents, she was certain they were happy to meet her. But as the next hour advanced, she began to think they would have been happy to meet whatever woman was visiting with Josh. From the hints they let fall, it was clear he hadn't introduced any girlfriends to his parents lately, and they'd begun to wonder if he was ever going to meet anyone at all.

Kristen, a tall woman with carefully applied lipstick and a coordinated pants outfit, was outgoing and friendly. Josh's father was a quiet man, given to an occasional dry observation. He liked to read to Hannah, his dark hair and more Asian countenance contrasting with her blond, childish looks as they peered over a page. When they were engrossed in *A Little Princess*, and Chloe was setting up chess pieces to play with Kristen, Josh touched Amy's arm.

"I have something for you," he said quietly.

Curious, she followed him down a hallway and turned into a large, comfortable library. Two computers, several bookshelves, and a wide white worktable established it as an office, a space so neat even the paperclips were in a little magnetic container. Since the late sunlight shining in made the room warm, Josh stepped to a window and pushed it open. Instantly, a mobile above the table slowly pivoted, its delicate metal arms catching the light. Pale white birds of folded paper moved with solemn grace.

"How pretty," she said.

"Those are my cranes," he said. "In Japan, the crane symbolizes peace and hope, like the dove does here."

"Did you fold them all?" she asked. She counted thirteen.

He nodded, walking to his desk. While he opened a drawer, she looked around again, noticing how high-tech the office was. There were packages of computer games, layout marketing posters, and several dozen marked boxes in a filing system along one wall. The Girl Funn logo was everywhere. On the center table was an intricate map with icons and hazards drawn in, creating a make-believe land where a computer figure could travel. She was impressed, and intrigued.

"Did you say you design computer games for girls?" she asked.

"And kids' learning programs, for libraries and such. My operations base is in California, but I collaborate with experts all over the country. We were lucky. We hit the market just as it exploded. I was planning to move our base to Minneapolis, but then Shannon died, and I've put things on hold while I concentrate on the girls."

He must be incredibly busy. She could hardly believe he could run a whole company from this office, but even then the fax started running in the corner. Josh didn't seem to notice. He was reaching in another drawer and pulling out a small white paper shape.

"Here," he said, holding it out to her.

She lifted the palm-sized canoe and held it to the light, marveling at the intricate folds that kept the paper rigid and strong. He'd written "Hope" on the bow of the boat, in tiny letters.

"I thought you'd like to launch a substitute hope canoe, so you can save your real one."

As she gazed at the little canoe, something crumpled inside her, making her feel vulnerable. More than anything, he was asking her to hope, and in a subtle way, he was asking her to hope for him. She didn't trust herself to look up.

"I don't know if I should accept this," she said.

"It's only paper."

But she shook her head, turning to gaze at the sunlight on the river valley. She sensed when Josh came to stand behind her, and then he put his hands on her shoulders, sending a cool sensation along her nerve endings so that she almost shivered. For a long moment she thought he was going to speak, but as the silence stretched out she knew he was trying to tell her something more powerful than words. It was as if he were telling her that he had more to give her—hope. Shared silence. A paper canoe. And family in the other room. Crazy almost-kisses and clapping games.

The *L* word.

FIVE

They got the bird out that night after Amy left. It took a broom, the tool kit, the ladder, towels, and the toilet plunger, but they triumphed. When Josh told Amy about it on the phone the next morning, she smiled as she imagined him and his dad hauling the dryer forward so he could crawl behind it to undo the vent. When the bird flew into the laundry room, the girls shrieked and hit the floor. Kristen finally threw a towel over the bird and took it outside. Craziest of all, when they finally released it, the bird flew to the vent and nearly made it back inside.

"So we need a pet," Josh finished. "Want to help us pick it out?"

"When are you going?"

"Later today. You could come with us and stay for a swim and dinner."

Amy knew even before she checked her calendar that it wasn't going to work. She sat at her desk on the second-floor office of her home, surrounded by pamphlets and catalogues, maps and correspondence, and tried not to feel totally swamped. She was supposed to be at the lake in an hour, helping Rex with a half-day canoe trip, and she still had two letters to finish. Swiveling in her chair, she wrapped her fingers in the coils of the phone cord.

"Sorry," she said. "I can't get away."

"We could wait until tomorrow. I could fly up and get you."

She felt even worse. "Tomorrow's no good either. The rest of this week's all booked."

There was a silence from his end of the line. "Are you trying to tell me something?"

Her stomach dove deep. "Only that I have a job. I do have to work, you know. I may not be racking up my first million, but I don't want to starve, either."

She heard a rapping noise from his end and couldn't tell if he was tapping a pencil or if one of the girls was hammering in the background. It was true, she argued with herself. She *did* have to work. Home Trail Outfitters depended on her.

"Josh?"

"I'm here. So when's good for you? Saturday? Sunday?"

She swiveled back to take another look at her calendar, and realized every square had scribbling in it. It wasn't as if she had holes in her life, just waiting to be filled. If she was going to make room for personal time, something else would have to give. She made a decision.

"Saturday," she said.

"Great. Do you want to have a picnic with me and the kids, or should you and I do something together?"

Though she was longing to have some time alone with Josh, she didn't feel comfortable telling him to leave his children behind. "Let's have a picnic," she said.

At the Nadja Ice Rink that Saturday, the double doors to the foyer were propped open, and a few families were going in and out, some with skates over their shoulders. The faint mustiness she always associated with ice rinks and gyms met Amy even before she fully entered the rink, and it gave her a twinge of excitement. She'd been looking forward to seeing the girls skate, so she was dismayed to see Chloe sitting on a bench in the otherwise deserted lacing-up area, her father nowhere in sight. The tips of her skates just barely touched the black rubber floor matting, and the cheerfulness of her pink leggings contrasted with her gloomy expression.

"Hi. What's up?" Amy asked.

"I got kicked out of my lesson."

Counting music on Monday, this was the second time in a week that Josh's eldest daughter had been kicked out of a class, and Amy could no longer think it was mere chance. The girl's attitude, even when she sat without speaking, rivaled that of a porcupine with a bad hair day, and she knew she'd have to be careful. From the other day when Chloe didn't play the clapping game with her, Amy already guessed Chloe didn't like her much. Amy drew closer, looked down at the girl's white skates, and saw that the laces on one were in a monstrous tangle.

"Do you need help taking these off?" Amy asked.

"Dad said to try to do it myself."

"Is he watching Hannah?"

"Yeah."

Amy detected so much gloom in the monosyllable

that she felt her heart stir in sympathy. It was hard to believe this frowning, sullen girl was the same one who had cared so deeply for the trapped bird, and who had swam so peacefully in the inner tube. Mercurial, Amy thought. It had to be hard bouncing between emotional extremes all the time.

"My skates used to get pretty tangled," Amy said. "Let's see if I can help."

She knelt down and propped the blade of the skate between her knees, feeling cold drops absorb into her jeans. After pushing her loose blond hair back over her shoulder with a quick twist, she picked at the knot with her short fingernails until finally it was clear.

"Thanks," Chloe said quietly.

Encouraged, Amy started on the other skate while Chloe unlaced the first.

"Do you want to tell me why you got kicked out?"

"The teacher said if we goofed around, we had to get off the ice. I thought she'd give us a warning or something."

"So you were goofing around?"

"I was just doing this," Chloe said. She made a prissy face and squeezed her fingers together as if pressing the bulb on an invisible perfume bottle. Amy remembered a previous reference to the skating teacher's musk, and let out a laugh.

"Oh, you're a scamp."

Chloe looked up through her glasses and gave a sheepish grin that was a lot like Josh's. Amy was secretly captivated.

"Anyway," the girl said, frowning again, "Dad's pretty mad."

Her father at that minute was walking into the changing area, accompanied by Hannah in her skates and a tall, dark-haired woman in a black skating outfit, also in her skates. The small area quickly filled with people helping their children in and out of skates. Amy thought Josh didn't see her on the floor because he showed no sign of recognition as he pointed Hannah toward Chloe, then turned to give his full attention to the dark-haired woman.

"Hi, Hannah," Amy said.

"Hi." The little girl sat next to her sister and smiled when Amy automatically started to help her with her skates. "We got hockey sticks at the end, Chloe, and I was really good. You missed out." Then to Amy, she said: "Do you have a tissue?"

Amy absently patted her pockets and handed one to her. She wasn't trying to listen, but she couldn't help overhearing Josh and the woman, who was obviously the skating instructor. They were a mere twenty feet away, and the woman was making no effort to keep her voice down. In fact, she was laughing and flirting in such an extroverted manner that a couple of the other parents in the room glanced in their direction.

Amy concentrated on Hannah's skates, unlooping the laces from the metal catches, but her ears burned when one of the instructor's lame jokes was followed by Josh's mellow laughter.

"Can't you stop her?" Chloe whispered.

Startled, Amy looked up and saw Chloe watching her father and the instructor with the intensity of an attack dog. Chloe gave her a little shove on the shoulder. "Go," she whispered.

Amy's heart gave one lurch of uncertainty. Then she rose and smoothed her hands down the seat of her jeans. What was she supposed to do? She had to walk around other skaters and past the end of a bench, but finally she stood beside Josh. He glanced in her direction just as the instructor gave his arm a friendly, intimate squeeze and a waft of perfume almost made Amy choke with laughter.

Casually, Josh put more space between himself and the other woman and smiled a greeting at Amy.

"Patricia, this is Amy Larkspur. Patricia's the girls' skating teacher."

"So you're Amy," Patricia said. "It's a pleasure. Do you skate?"

"Only in the winter," she said.

Patricia gave her a big smile. "You should try it in the summer some time. I've got to run. Level two's starting. See you later, Josh."

Patricia headed back toward the rink, her black outfit accentuating her striking figure as she moved out over the ice. Amy glanced up sideways at Josh, waiting for a cue from him. He was watching her, too, and when he saw her curiosity, he chuckled and ran a hand through his hair.

"You have just been registered on the grapevine. In case you weren't already there," he said.

Amy felt her cheeks growing warmer and started back toward Chloe and Hannah. "I never cared much about the grapevine."

"It's going to care a little about you, though," he said with an edge.

She wasn't sure she heard him correctly over the noise. "What?"

"Never mind."

Chloe and Hannah were already wearing their shoes, and Hannah was very carefully forming loops on one of her sneakers.

"I am *not* going to apologize," Chloe said.

Amy saw the girl's defensive attitude had returned full force.

"We'll talk about this outside." Josh's voice held a clear warning.

His change in tone was so complete and seemed so out of proportion, that Amy's gaze shot upward. His expression had darkened with stern authority as he observed his daughter.

Chloe swung her skates, and they hit loudly against the bench with a gouging noise.

"Chloe!" Josh said sharply.

"I didn't mean to—"

"Wait outside," he said.

Chloe jutted out her chin, clutched her skates against her chest, and pushed past her father toward the door. With visible restraint, Josh helped Hannah gather her things. Amy could see the tension in his clenched jaw and sensed that he was both embarrassed and angry. She glanced around, but the other parents didn't seem to notice the exchange, and a girl in a red sweater said a nice good-bye to Hannah as they headed out.

Amy wanted to ask Josh what was going on, but she never got the chance. Even before they reached Josh's car, Chloe and Hannah began to argue about whose turn it was to sit in the front, and Chloe shoved Hannah so hard the six-year-old fell against the side of the car and started to cry.

"That's it!" Josh said. "You're in the way back, Chloe."

"But it's *my* turn to sit in the front," Chloe protested.

"Come here," Josh said to Hannah, ignoring Chloe. "Are you all right?"

Hannah, who was clearly trying to hold back her

tears, put her arms around Josh's neck and squeezed tight as he lifted her up into a hug.

"You *always* take her side," Chloe said. "You *never* believe me."

Josh merely swiveled so his back was toward Chloe and continued to comfort Hannah.

Chloe reached for the handle to the back door of the car and tugged on it fiercely, even after it became obvious that the door was locked. "I *hate* this stupid car!"

She gave another wrench that was so hard her hand slipped and she went flying backward. She would have fallen hard on the asphalt except Amy was there to catch her. Chloe quickly pulled free from Amy's hands, saying "Leave me alone."

Amy was shocked by how quickly it all happened. Josh turned his face to glare at Chloe, and Amy was afraid he was about to scold Chloe for being rude when Hannah said in a little voice, "She can sit in the front."

"Oh, great," Josh said, and let out an exasperated laugh.

"I'm okay," Hannah said, getting down from Josh's arms. "You can have the front, Chloe."

Josh ran a hand through his hair so it stood up above his ear, then planted both fists on his hips. He looked completely harried, totally unlike the cool, reserved man she'd learned to expect. Amy didn't know what to say. The children of her experience had never demonstrated the degree of hostility that Chloe seemed to have, and the last thing Amy wanted to do was say something that might undermine Josh's authority.

"Let's both sit in the way back," Chloe said.

"Okay," the little girl replied.

And without further complaint, both girls climbed

in the unlocked front door and scrambled over the seats to the rear-facing backseat of the station wagon.

Amy let out an enormous sigh of relief. "Wow."

"Sorry about that." Josh reached to unlock the middle door, then tossed the girls' skates on the floor of the car.

"She seems so angry," Amy said. As long as they stayed outside the car, she doubted the girls could hear them talking.

"Tell me about it. It's been one thing after another all morning. And she was impossible with Patricia. She distracted every other kid in the skating group with her antics. She just can't settle down."

"What can you do for her?"

He inhaled sharply and frowned. "It's driving me nuts," he said. "She has all these mixed emotions. She just has to learn to express them in an appropriate way, and she has to realize she isn't going to get attention for behaving badly."

"That's why you ignored her?" Amy asked. "I mean, when you were holding Hannah?"

He gave a grim smile. "I was trying to at least."

Amy looked through the back window of the car, to where Hannah and Chloe were playing a game with Popsicle sticks. They looked peaceful enough, but Amy knew now that they could erupt into a fight at any time. She didn't like to admit it, but all that emotion made her uncomfortable. It made her feel inept. She didn't know how she would have handled that situation if the girls had been her own daughters.

"So are you ready for this picnic?" he asked.

"Do you think they'll be okay?"

He was watching her strangely, and Amy felt her stomach knot up.

"They'll be okay," he said. "I promised them a backward picnic, with dessert first, so I thought we'd start with ice cream. Is that okay with you?"

"Sure."

He opened the door for her and she slid into the front seat, keenly aware she was sitting in the spot his daughters had fought about only minutes before.

"Is Amy coming with us?" Chloe called from the backseat.

Josh sat in the driver's seat. "I told you she was."

Amy glanced sideways at him, but he merely checked out the rearview mirror and began backing the car into the lot. When a rush of air-conditioning came out of the vents, she adjusted the one before her so it was aimed at her neck. Even as she tried to relax, she could tell that Josh was still wound tight, especially when he turned on a country station and didn't try to talk over the music.

All they needed now was to end up at Mindy's. Fate couldn't be that sadistic, not when there were three other far more conspicuous ice cream parlors in Harmony. Five minutes later, Josh took a right and pulled into the familiar lot of Mindy's ice cream stand.

Oh, boy. Just what she needed.

Mindy's was named after the owner, a small, pleasant woman who made the ice cream from her own secret recipe, with nothing but fresh eggs, cream, and natural flavors. The ice cream was always delicious, the service homey and polite, but Amy had avoided going there all summer because Mindy was Andy Kyle's mother, and Amy would bet ten gallons of Rocky Road that Mindy knew exactly how badly Aim Larkspur had broken Andy Kyle's heart.

Josh got Hannah and Chloe out of the way back,

and the four of them strolled up to the walk-up window. The place was busy, with four or five teenagers working in bright red vests and half a dozen occupying picnic tables on the grass lawn. From behind their server, Mindy gave them a big smile and then looked again at Amy.

"Why, Amy!" Mindy said. "Haven't seen you in ages. How are things?"

"Fine, Mindy. Thanks. How are you?"

"Not bad. Andy decided to take that teaching position down in the Cities, you know. We're hoping he decides to move back here when it's over."

"He told me it's going well. I'm sure it's a great opportunity for him."

"We were kind of hoping things would work out for you two. But you never can tell. Is this gentleman with you? Don't be shy about introducing him."

Amy mentally groaned and looked at Josh. He smiled with polite interest, but she could see him putting pieces together. He extended his hand to Mindy and introduced himself. "And these are my daughters, Chloe and Hannah. We've heard great things about your ice cream. This is our first time here."

That was all the encouragement Mindy needed. She invited Chloe and Hannah back for a tour, then offered to make them a couple of her own sampler sundaes.

Josh leaned in the doorway and gave Amy a thoughtful look. "You're well-connected in Harmony."

She blushed and looked to be sure Mindy was out of earshot. "I dated her son a while back."

"So I gathered. Is he in the ice-cream business?"

"He's a vet."

"Does he happen to be your basic, decent guy?" Josh asked.

Her blush deepened even more. "Something like that."

"I see."

Amy doubted he did, but she couldn't see explaining it to him there, with Andy's mother hovering in the background. With relief, she saw the tour was over, and with a couple of good-byes, they were leading Hannah and Chloe to a vacant picnic table in the shade. Hannah began eating with relish, but Chloe looked at Amy and slowly licked chocolate off her spoon.

"Are you dating my father?" Chloe asked.

Amy glanced at Josh, hoping he'd step in with an answer. He merely watched her.

"I like him," Amy said. "We haven't gone to dinner and a movie, but we've been getting together some. Is that what you mean?"

"Have you kissed him?" Chloe asked.

Amy swallowed hard, and again looked at Josh. His lips were widening slowly in an amused, lazy smile, and his eyes were warm with humor. He took a slow lick of his vanilla ice cream and lifted his eyebrows.

"Well?" he asked.

Even Hannah stopped eating to look at Amy.

"What makes you ask?" Amy said to Chloe.

"My mom said to tell her if Dad was ever kissing anyone else," Chloe said.

"Oh, Chloe," Amy said.

"Hey, bug," Josh said, and pulled Chloe closer to him on the bench so he could keep his arm around her.

If Amy had felt uncertain of what to say before, now she had zero clue. Even Hannah stopped eating her ice cream to see what her dad would say.

Josh was good; Amy would give him that. He talked to Chloe in a calm voice about Shannon, and how it must be hard not having her to talk to anymore, especially when something was confusing.

"It isn't so much confusing," Chloe said. "It's that I don't know who to tell things to."

"Why not tell things to me?" Josh asked.

"How can I tell you things about yourself?" Chloe said.

He looked perplexed.

Amy smiled. "I think I get it. You were supposed to report to your mom about your dad, but now she's not there to report to, is that it?"

"Yeah," said Chloe, as if this were obvious.

"Why not tell your grandmother?" Amy suggested. "Your ideas about your father are pretty important, and she knows him well. Couldn't you tell her?"

"Wait a minute here," Josh said.

But Chloe ignored him. "I think I could." Her expression lightened slowly. "That might work."

"Me too," Hannah said. "I can ask Grandma why Daddy doesn't wear pajamas."

Chloe covered her mouth and both girls began to giggle.

"Hey, you monsters," their father said. He extended both hands as claws and then began to tickle them mercilessly. Chloe and Hannah laughed and screamed, and Hannah's ice cream tipped off the table onto the grass.

Amy watched from across the picnic table, while her mind turned over the information that Josh didn't wear pajamas. Did that mean he slept in boxers, or in briefs? Or in the nude? She shifted on the picnic bench, feeling physically aware of him even though he wasn't concentrating on her at all.

Get a grip, Aim, she warned herself. The man's focused on his daughters. Try not to lust after him over melting ice cream.

Josh finally finished tickling the girls when they backed beyond reach and had to gasp to catch their breath.

"I have to go to the bathroom," Hannah said.

"Chloe, you take her," Josh said.

"Do I have to?"

"It's right over there." He pointed to a door on the side of the building.

"Do I have to put paper on the seat?" Hannah said.

"Chloe will help you," Josh said. "Go on."

As his daughters started over toward the building, Josh covered his face in his hands and groaned. "Am I insane, or is my mother about to hear that I don't wear pajamas?"

Amy smiled at him and let the humor of it slide down through her with her last spoonful of strawberry ice cream. "She may, in fact, become privy to that information."

"I have you to thank for that."

Amy grinned and leaned her elbows on the picnic table, avoiding a sticky smudge of old ice cream. Josh's hair was mussed over his forehead, and when he put up a hand to smooth it down, the sunlight made a deep shadow under his hand, just for a moment. His even teeth showed between his lips when he gave a one-sided grin, and a deep line appeared in his tanned cheek. She felt a pull of attraction, and it made her want to lean across the table to kiss him.

"When are you going to ask what I wear instead of pajamas?" he asked.

Oh, God. "This is a family place."

"I could give you a multiple choice."

"Let's just say you wear cotton and leave it at that."

He grinned, impressed. "Close enough. How many days has it been since I kissed you?" he asked. "Fifty? Sixty?"

She laughed. "A few."

"This is not a good thing."

"This is reality."

"Let's make a vow," he said melodramatically, "that before the sun sets tonight we kiss three times."

"You've been watching too many kids' videos," she said.

He propped his chin on his fist with deceptive innocence. "Then why don't I have a G-rating right now?"

"What do you—" But before she could ask what he meant, his wicked, seductive expression made heat spiral through her. Her own hormones kicked in at a rating way beyond PG. "You enjoy this, don't you?"

"It's torment," he said. "I want that kiss promise. At least two kisses."

"Your daughters are emerging from the women's room."

"One kiss. Make the promise, or I can't be held responsible for what happens."

"They both look like they've been crying."

"Make the promise, I say." He growled.

"Hannah has toilet paper trailing out of her pants."

By the time Josh finally turned to see Hannah and Chloe, Hannah was crying for real and Chloe was stubbornly telling her to be quiet.

"Time to go," Josh said, pulling the toilet paper out of Hannah's waistband. In a matter of minutes, he had them both in the car, each with a wet wipe for her hands and face. He closed the door and stood looking over the roof of the car at Amy. Rueful exasperation had worn him down once again, but he seemed to take it for granted that Amy's sense of humor was still intact.

"You know," she said, "maybe this isn't the best day for me to join you guys for a picnic."

The light instantly vanished from his expression. "Don't say that."

She could feel her conviction growing in proportion to her fear of disappointing him. "No, really. The girls have obviously had a rough day so far. They'd probably be happy to just hang out with you."

"They would, that's true, but all they really need is a little lunch and they'll be fine."

Amy eyed him skeptically.

"Listen," he said, "we're not happy all the time, Amy. It isn't anything to be ashamed of."

"I'm not saying it is. But am I supposed to make things worse?"

"You don't make things worse."

She let out a brief laugh and moved in back of the car so the girls wouldn't be able to hear her. Josh followed and lowered his voice.

"I don't want to get into a big analysis of the girls' problems. They're just kids. And they're going to be okay. Let's just have some lunch and kick around the playground."

Amy glanced at the busy parking lot of Mindy's, and sighed heavily. Part of her longed to go with him, but a deeper part of her empathized with Chloe and Hannah and sensed that their distress really might have something to do with her. How could she be playing a kissing game with their father while the girls were falling apart? Josh had a complicated life already, and his first priority would always be to his girls, or should be. Amy didn't see how she fit into that. Part of her was afraid too. What if she tried to befriend his daughters, and they ended up hating her? She didn't want to risk that.

When she looked back at Josh, his eyes had an expression she'd never seen before: closed and knowing.

"We're too complicated for you, aren't we?" he said, his voice flat.

Amy felt cold fingers tug on her heart. She shook her head. "No. But this might not be the right time."

"For us?"

She pressed her lips inward and looked down at the dusty bumper of the car. The tension between them was so thick that she found it hard to breathe.

"I refuse to have this conversation in the parking lot of Mindy's ice cream," he said. "Come with us for the picnic and we'll get a chance to talk."

She shook her head. "The girls don't want me, Josh. They haven't said it in so many words, but they shouldn't have to. And I can't have a serious conversation when we're being interrupted all the time. I'm sorry, Josh. It'll have to be another time."

"But why? You're making a problem out of nothing."

Her eyes flashed to his. "Don't ever say there's nothing," she said.

"All right. I'm sorry."

"These are real issues, Josh."

"I know. I'm sorry. I'm just frustrated that you won't come with us."

But she couldn't. All her gut instincts told her she couldn't go with him and his contentious daughters, not now. It would be one thing if she had to, if they were part of her job or part of her family, but—

She broke off on the thought, even more confused.

How could she possibly think of Josh in terms of family, even hypothetically?

He cursed under his breath, and then set his hand on Amy's arm, his eyes dark with concern. "Okay. All right."

She withdrew slowly, trying to chase after an elusive clue that would give her the secret to her feelings.

"It would be pretty easy for you to walk away, wouldn't it?" he said, his voice low and dead serious.

She shivered and tried to find something in his expression that would tell her how much she mattered to him. His eyes were watchful and tense, but his lips had a trace of a smile that could almost convince her he didn't care. He was trying to make it easy for her, she realized.

But that wasn't what she wanted either. She knew if she cared less, she could make herself join him for the picnic; but because she did care about him and his daughters, she couldn't make herself go. Completely backward. She closed her eyes against the first tightening of a headache.

"Josh," she said, opening her eyes, "I can't explain it."

"No problem," he said, and his smile widened a bit more. "We'll just try another day. I'll drop you back at your car."

"Josh—"

But he simply waved her into her seat, then crossed around to his door, and in the cheeriest manner possible, he drove her back to her car at the ice rink, dropped her off, and drove off with the girls.

SIX

"Then I stir, or I don't stir?" Amy asked.

As if she were next door and not six time zones away, Amy's mother's voice came clearly over the phone. "Don't stir. Just watch those little therapeutic bubbles of milk and wait for the chocolate to ooze up."

Amy stared at the milk, sugar, and chocolate squares in her pot, half squinting because the light over the stove shone down so brightly. Over low heat, the milk was slowly turning into thick white bubbles that rose around the chocolate squares until, in another minute, they covered the chocolate in a merry swirl. The scent that wafted up was warm and delicious, offsetting the midnight darkness that was thick and oppressive beyond her kitchen windows.

"Are you sure you were up?" Amy asked, feeling a last twinge of guilt.

"It's seven here," her mother said. "I've been up for an hour and had my walk already. Nigel's having his tea right across the table from me. Say hello, Nigel."

Amy heard Nigel's obliging Irish brogue in the

background, and smiled. She could almost see her mother pointing the phone in his direction, the breakfast table spread with linen, china, little pots of jelly, and rolls. Then her mother was right back on the line.

"Did you really clean your oven?"

"And the refrigerator," Amy said.

"This is serious."

"I know. I'm wired. I can't sleep. All I want is chocolate."

Amy's mother sighed, and then came the noise of a rustling newspaper. "Maybe you should write down the fudge recipe this time," she said. "And not lose it. Don't you still have it around from the Andy days?"

"This man is *nothing* like Andy."

Her mother made a whistling noise.

"And besides, it never works unless you're talking me through it. The bubbles are turning brown now. Do I stir?"

"Do not stir."

There was a shuffling noise on Amy's porch, and then a knock. She froze, then instinctively checked the clock: exactly midnight.

"There's somebody here," Amy whispered.

"It's about time," her mother said. "Now the two of you can thrash it out."

"What makes you think it's him and not some burglar?" Amy asked, peeking through the dining room door toward the front door. Her heart was beating as if the big bad wolf were growling out there.

"Please. Would you go open the door?" said her mother. "I'll hold."

Standing on the porch, Josh couldn't believe that he was actually there at midnight, and that her lights were on. An awake, nonhostile person would at least check the door. So then, where was she?

She was going to think he was absolutely insane, whether she answered or not. But at least if she thought he was insane, she'd be bothering to think about him. That would only be fair, since he'd been wound up and out of his mind ever since the Mindy's fiasco.

First the light came on over the door, then one eye showed as she peeped through the living room window, and finally he saw her open the door. Halfway. She wasn't exactly smiling, either. In fact, she held a cordless phone as if prepared to dial 911.

"I hope I'm not intruding," he said.

Though he tried to sound cool, he couldn't help devouring the sight of her. She was wearing old cut-off jeans, frayed just above her knees, and a black sleeveless tank top that hung down to her thighs. Faded letters in the center of the shirt read: BABE WAS HERE and sported a giant blue ox-hoof print below. She'd knotted her wild blond curls in a twist that only slightly resembled the formal hair-do she'd had at Lee and Briana's wedding, for now the curls along her neck were dampened with sweat, and several tendrils along her forehead were similarly askew. Though her attire showed healthy signs of grit and wear, the clothes clung with tantalizing softness to her slender figure, while a thin gold chain around her neck rested in the crevice at the base of her throat and glinted in the light.

When he'd fantasized about being alone with her, he'd pictured her in something more seductive, but not even his fantasy could rival the impact she was having on him now. How was he going to concentrate on all the things he'd rehearsed to say?

"Are you going to let me in?" he asked.

Without smiling, she opened the door wider. "Be my intrusion. I mean, my *guest*," she said.

As he stepped into the living room, she hurried away, and as he watched her slender figure disappear into the kitchen, he inhaled deeply. The most intoxicating smell of chocolate was lacing the air, a scent so rich he actually hummed. Walking slowly, he followed the lure into the kitchen just as Amy said good-bye and hung up the phone.

"That was my mother," Amy said.

Not some guy. Good.

"Isn't it a little late for a phone call?" he asked, as if his appearance wasn't at all strange.

Amy reached for the dial on her stove and turned it off as she removed a pot from the burner. "It's morning in Dublin. They're already on tomorrow."

He knew well enough what it was like to calculate time zones for phone calls, since he'd done it often enough when Shannon was traveling.

"What did you call her for?"

"How do you know I called her?" she asked.

"Just a guess."

She was cutting a half-inch slice off a stick of butter, and he thought he saw the knife tremble when the yellow glob slipped onto the counter. She scooped up the soft butter with her fingers and dropped it in the pot with the chocolate mixture, and the quick, fluid gesture made him ache to lick her buttery fingers clean. *Get ahold of yourself, Kita.* When she turned to face him, he was totally unprepared for her honest, vulnerable expression.

"I called her because of you," she said.

A jolt of awareness shot through him, and he knew

tonight was going to cover a lot more than buttery fingers.

"What did you say about me?"

"We didn't get to the subtleties. We only got as far as the fudge recipe."

He glanced at the pot. "Don't you need to stir it?"

She let out a frustrated growl and reached for a paper towel to wipe her fingers. Then she crossed her arms over her chest.

"What are you doing here?" she demanded.

He liked her when she was peeved. He liked her when she was downright ornery. If he retraced all the mistakes from that afternoon, he'd be right back in an argument when all he wanted to do was take her in his arms and kiss her until all the doubt and annoyance vanished for good. *Improvise.* He allowed himself one step forward.

"My parents were over for dinner tonight," he said.

"And?"

"Hannah and Chloe begged them to stay for a sleep over. They do that now and then." He took another step closer, and the small space of the kitchen seemed to grow ten degrees warmer. He scratched his head, watching her for signs of awareness, but she kept her arms crossed and didn't move. Only a flicker at the back of her eyes warned him he'd better be careful.

"And then?" she asked.

"After the kids were sleeping, my father wanted me to tell him about our new bird. It's a parakeet named Rover." He lifted his eyebrows, but she wasn't smiling, so he continued. "All I could do was pace around the living room wishing they'd go to bed so I could be alone and think."

"Fascinating."

He was not encouraged. If this approach failed, he was going to be out on his ear. He took another step closer. This time she uncrossed her arms and casually leaned back into a corner of the counter, bracing a hand on either side of her.

"Then my mother, the genius—"

"Mothers are always smart."

"She said to me," he continued, "Why don't you go for a spin in that plane of yours?"

Amy's eyebrows lifted, and he could see by the necklace at the base of her throat that her heart was beating faster than normal. "Very insightful," she said.

"My father wanted to come with me."

For the first time that night, she smiled. "But you didn't let him."

"No," he said, and came one step closer so that his shoes were twelve inches from her bare feet.

Now he had her where he wanted her: backed into a corner, sweet and mussed and very, very alone. As the fudge was left to cool, he felt an intense heat coiling in his lower abdomen, and he realized that he'd been wanting her badly for a long time: through all the days of waiting until he'd see her again, through all those platonic moments over lemonade and ice cream. In the plane tonight he'd hardly let himself hope that she might be awake to answer the door. But now he was really there, and he wanted to savor every second, every inch of what was to come.

To hell with explanations. He set his hands over hers where they rested on the counter, and then slowly slid his palms up her bare, slender arms, until he came to the warm skin of her shoulders and the tension of her muscles. He rubbed a thumb under one shoulder strap of her top, and nearly lost his breath when he realized there was no bra strap beneath. His eyes shot to her black shirt, and the tell-tale points of her breasts were pressing through the fabric, almost hidden under the slight thickness of the blue lettering.

"Oh, God," he said. How the devil was he going to take this slow? How was he going to convince her he had to stay?

Amy tilted her face back and made an effort to unclench her jaw, but every fiber of her body was taut with the strain of being so close to him. The black- and sand-colored tones of his shirt gave his gray eyes a mysterious, liquid depth that mesmerized and unnerved her. She wasn't kidding when she'd said before that he gave her vertigo; if she weren't hanging on to the counter for dear life, she would swoon right to the floor. Or into his arms. Her body ached to be against his, but all he was doing so far was holding her shoulders and gazing at her like a wolf, the same big bad one she'd been afraid of.

He was the game master; she knew that. He could hold there and tease her until she thought she'd die, or she could take the initiative and turn the game backward on him. *Or is it just a game?*

"Close your eyes," she said.

His eyes narrowed into one long, piercing gaze, and then he closed them.

She licked her lips, praying it would work, and then she brought her lips an inch from his and stopped there, hovering, feeling his breath against her lips and knowing he must feel hers. Then she held tight to the counter behind her and leaned forward the last inch, like an arrow pulled taut in a bow to bring her lips against his.

With a curse he crushed her against him, and every

inch of her tense body soared to meet its mark. Deep inside, a spreading heat and hunger ignited everywhere with no hope of satisfaction except from him. She leaned into his kiss, heedless of any last reservations or shyness, and arched her body to bring her belly and breasts in full contact along the hard planes of his torso. At last, she thought. Twining her arms around his neck, she gasped as his lips began a trail of exquisite fire along her jaw and descended along her throat.

Faster, she silently urged him, but time seemed to slow tortuously and spread out, each second infused with sensation. His hands were lifting under her shirt and skimming upward along her back. The effect of his cool palms on her hot skin made her shiver, but she didn't feel cold. She moaned and pressed her closed eyes against the warmth of his neck, inhaling the masculine scent of his skin, the faint trace of sweat mixed with the cotton of his shirt.

His lips touched on her cheek and temple, while his hands continued an intoxicating, slow tour under her shirt. She could feel him pause, and then he stroked one hand along her rib cage and gently upward to meet the undercurve of her breast. Her knees went liquid on her, and she had to hold still while his thumb skimmed her breast and brushed lightly against her nipple.

A hot current of desire swept through her and she moaned with pleasure. Josh kissed her again, more fervently than before, and she could feel the strength of his arousal through his trousers as he pressed his body against hers and pinned her back against the counter. For a moment he remained pressed against her, and then with a quick shift of his weight, he lifted her up so she was sitting on the counter and he could stand between her knees.

Amy's whole body was almost painfully alive with wanting him. When she could feel him so close, separated from her only by the fabric of her shorts and his trousers, it almost made her wild. She tugged impatiently at his shirt, hoping he would help her pull it over his head to get rid of it, but he merely chuckled and tilted his face to look at her.

His eyes glowed with perceptive heat, and his elegant lips moved in a seductive half smile. He rested his hands on her waist, his thumbs gently massaging the skin above the waistband of her shorts.

"I happen to like these buttons," he said.

His voice was so deep and gravelly, it seemed to resonate down her own throat. She licked her lips. She brought her fingers forward to begin on the first button, but her concentration was suddenly broadsided by the stroking of his palms along her sides. As she finished the first button he paused, but when she began the second, his hands moved sensuously to establish command at the base of her breasts, and she involuntarily arched upward with a sharp intake of breath. With the gap afforded in the waistband of her shorts, he slipped one hand downward until she felt his fingertips reach the edge of her bikini underpants. If he chose to stroke the back of his fingers there, she would be helpless to withstand him. She could feel heat and moisture build at the apex of her legs.

"Next button, please," he said.

She swallowed hard and began working on the next button, but her fingers faltered. She had to stop while all her senses concentrated on the effect his hands were having on the more intimate regions of her body. Amy finally gave up altogether and rested her head against the cabinet behind her, leaving her neck and body deliciously subject to any touch he cared to give.

"Damn," he said, and with one quick movement, he shucked his shirt over his head. "You must have a bed somewhere in this place."

"Up the stairs. To the right. I mean, to the left. Make that straight ahead."

He chuckled and lifted her against him. She straddled her legs around his waist and left the navigating to him. She had more important pursuits, namely losing herself in the exquisite muscles that played under the tan skin of his shoulders. Why had she never seen him without his shirt on before? It seemed impossible that she'd been deprived of such incredible masculine beauty until now. And he'd willingly held back his most persuasive assests until now, despite all their disagreements.

This was *not* sex for fun, she'd have to remind him later.

He set her on the bed. She slipped out of her shorts, taking her underpants off, too, and sat up on the quilted coverlet wearing only her sleeveless shirt. Josh was ridding himself of shoes, socks, and trousers at impressive speed, until he was standing, naked and magnificent in the moonlight that came from the skylights above. They covered the entire ceiling, six of them, and half of them were cranked up to let in air through the screens.

He glanced up. "Nice skylights," he said.

"Don't tell me you came to admire the view."

"No," he said slowly, approaching over the bed. "I have only one view in mind."

She issued a low laugh. "That's really bad," she said, but she let him take the edge of her shirt and start pulling it upward.

If anything, the lull in the momentum had only increased her desire for him, and now she couldn't wait to feel him next to her, in her. He knelt before her where she sat on the coverlet, and she spread her fingers over the muscular planes of his chest, reveling in the heat of his smooth skin, the fine hairs that tapered down toward his waist. She could see the outline of his smile and the hooded passion in his eyes as his gaze traveled over her body.

"What is this, here?" he asked softly. His finger lingered on a small scar over her left breast, and she glanced down at herself.

"When I was swimming once as a kid, I impaled myself on a nail at the end of a dock as I tried to get out."

"Ouch," he said, and leaned nearer to kiss the scar.

She brushed her cheek against his hair, and then, when his kisses began to gain urgency and his mouth explored her breasts, she felt the vertigo ride her hard, and she involuntarily arched backward. In another moment she leaned back on the bed, bringing him with her.

Every inch of her skin burned where she came in contact with him, and while she'd tried to match his slow pace earlier, now she couldn't bear to be patient any longer.

With a twinge of uncertainty, she brought her fingers to his face and touched his jaw. "Did you bring a condom?" she whispered.

He smiled at her in the dim light. "You read my mind." He'd left his trousers next to the bed, and she watched as he reached into the pocket and withdrew the foil. Something about his consideration touched her deeply and added still another dimension to her feelings for him.

In a moment he was beside her again, and with deft fingers he smoothed the hair back from her face, then kissed her eyebrow and the sensitive skin of her temple. She could feel his hard, hot body against the length of hers, could feel every famished cell of her body reaching toward him. Her breasts ached with a kind of maddening fullness, and he seemed to know instinctively that she wanted him to touch her there. Shifting her beneath him, he lowered his head and circled one sensitive nipple with his tongue, teasing the taut peak until she almost cried out.

She shifted against him, guiding his arousal toward her sensitive folds, longing to have him in her.

"I can go slow," he said gruffly.

"I can't."

For an instant he didn't move, and his eyes just inches from hers nearly closed with the intensity of his control, then he seemed to burst with fierce energy. He moved over her with long, deep thrusts, feeding a blaze inside her that matched only what she had dreamed could be possible. Her earlier experiences were nothing against the power she felt burning in her now, and she gasped as the urgency of his desire charged through her.

Shattered were all her former concepts of ecstasy and fulfillment. The explosion that rocked through her blasted not only her body, but her entire universe. *How can he do this incredible thing with me?* Even as a billion crystalline stars shattered around her, leaving everything liquid and free, she knew deep within her that a part of her, a wandering, adventurous, formerly wild

part of her, was now inextricably fixed upon the man in
her arms.

Hours later, she awoke to find him tucking the quilt
under her chin.

"All right?" he whispered.

She stretched with heavy-limbed pleasure and snuggled more closely into his arms. She liked the feel of his
bare skin against hers, especially where her back was
lined against his warm torso. His arm came intimately
around her waist and lightly stoked once down her
belly. A trail of goosebumps rose across her pelvis, and
that was all it took for a new flash of desire to stir in her
gut. Devil, she thought. She licked her lips, keeping her
eyes closed.

With her left hand, she reached behind her for his
hip, then reached lower to stretch her fingers wide
along his muscular thigh.

He pressed a kiss along the back of her neck. "I
thought if you were awake, maybe we could talk."

"Is it very urgent?" she asked.

He shifted slightly, and she could feel his hard
arousal press against the back of her legs.

"Not as urgent as other matters," he said.

"There is the issue of the responsible adult, after
all."

He slid his hand slowly down her belly again, causing the muscles of her abdomen to clench automatically. "Say sex for fun and I'll throw your fudge out the
window. Or something worse."

She couldn't resist. "Sex for fun."

"You asked for it," he said, and with one deft move
he was on top of her, pinning her thighs beneath the

weight of one leg. She laughed and instinctively tried to shift free, but he pulled both of her wrists together above her head and held them against the pillow. Once he'd established the position he wanted her in, he loosened his hold to the barest pressure, so she could slip free if she chose to or remain a willing captive. She gazed up at his face and saw the rectangles of the skylights behind him outlining his silhouette. How could he be so strong and gentle at the same time? She lay still and forced her muscles to relax, even when she realized he was using his free hand to trace a line down her cheek to her jaw.

She licked her lips again, feeling thirsty everywhere.

"Do you always have a condom in your pants pocket?" she asked, hoping to keep her voice conversational.

"No," he said reasonably. "Though I happen to have a couple more. Do you keep any spares in your bedroom?"

She could feel him roll his hand so the backs of his fingers began to move down her throat. She felt the warmth start between her legs, and her nipples grew taut with expectation.

"Well?" he asked.

"No."

He trailed his hand off along her shoulder, taking a detour away from her breasts, and she pressed her lips together to keep from moaning.

"What is it?" he asked.

"Nothing."

He began to trail his knuckles back toward her breasts, and she arched slightly, unconsciously encouraging him. A deep grumble of amusement came from his throat.

"Do you have any idea how incredible you are?" he said.

She smiled with pleasure at the compliment, and just then he brought his hand against her nipple. She inhaled sharply at his touch, and then it was his turn to moan.

"Come here," he said, releasing her to pull her on top of him.

This time he pulled the clasp free from her hair, and her blond curls curtained around her face. When he kissed her, twining his fingers in her hair, she felt pure, utter abandon rip through her, and her need was more than she could bear. She could tell that his body, like her own, was still primed from before and hungry with the expectation of how good it was going to be. They came together soon, perfectly matched, and afterward she was again astonished that fires of gold could ignite every inch of her.

How could her own body feel such intense pleasure in such different ways? Would it be a little different each time she made love with Josh? A distant warning sounded in the back of her mind, reminding her there was no promise of a future with him, but she banished the concept and concentrated instead on the pure, sated pleasure that warmed her.

She felt his fingers softly stroking her hair and heard the regular sound of his breathing as she snuggled against him. Above, the stars were still bright pinpoints through the skylights, but the faintest lightening of the sky was tinting the black with purple. It would be dawn in another hour.

Amazing to think the world was still turning, she thought. It seemed to have been blown off course for a while.

"I guess we caught up on those kisses," he said. "All three."

She had to think for a moment before she remembered his promise about kisses before yesterday's sunset, and then she shifted slightly so she could look into his face. She couldn't quite make out his expression, merely the shadowy planes of his jaw and nose and forehead, but she could tell he was ready to talk.

"For such a reserved person," he said, "you certainly know when to let loose."

His comment surprised her. "I'm not that reserved," she said.

"Then how come there are so many things I still don't know about you?"

"Like what?"

He slowly brushed a hair back from her forehead, and when he answered his voice was deceptively light. "Like what happened with Mindy's son. Like how come my daughters frighten you."

Amy felt the bed lose its legs and crash sideways, or at least seem to. With her heart thudding painfully, she withdrew from him and sat up on the bed, bringing an edge of the quilt to hold against her. After one long, tense moment, he pulled the light switch, and a soft glow spread through the green shade of the small lamp, pushing the shadows toward the corners of the room. She could see he was frowning at her, waiting, and for an instant she wished he would just turn the light off again and let her sleep.

Don't be a coward, Aim. She made herself look him straight in the eye. "Your daughters don't frighten me."

"Well, if it isn't fear exactly, it's something."

"I've never dated anybody who had kids before," she said.

His slow smile lifted one corner of his mouth, and he shifted over to rest on one elbow. His chest was in shadow, but the lamp behind him sent a line of light along his shoulder and side, outlining his magnificent body and making her wish all of their relationship could be as simple and powerful as what they had just shared.

"I hope that's not the only difference between me and the other men you've dated," he said.

She smiled uneasily. "No."

"You like kids in general, don't you?"

"Yes," she said. "I can't wait for Cottie and Sean to have their baby so I can be an aunt. I love kids."

She saw him smooth his palm slowly over a wrinkle in the sheet, and knew he was thinking. "Hannah and Chloe don't dislike you," he said. "Chloe was afraid it was her fault that you didn't come with us for the picnic."

"I'm sorry, Josh."

He shook his head. "No. You were right not to come. They did relax once I dropped you off." He exhaled a long breath. "I don't know what to make of it. Suppose we leave the girls out of it for now." He looked back up at her, and his rakish smile changed the subtle tension between them. "What happened with the basic, decent guy? The one I'm nothing like?"

"That's Andy. Mindy's son."

"Andy, then. How long did you know him? Why'd you break up?"

She looked at Josh's eyes, and then gazed toward the windows. While she absently noted that the sky was turning more violet, she thought about Andy. Josh wasn't just asking to be curious; she knew that now. In some way, he really cared.

"I've always known Andy." Her quiet voice was

clear and soft in the dimly lit room. "I can't remember when I didn't. He taught me how to spit off the bridge when I was six, and once he beat up my brother, Sean, for teasing me." She smiled. "Talk about backward loyalties."

Josh didn't smile. "Of course, you fell in love with him."

Amy shook her head. "I didn't love him. I mean, I did. I do. But as a friend." She gazed down at her fingers in the quilt and unclenched them enough to get more comfortable. She shifted to pull her knees up in front of her and crossed her arms over the top of them. "It still makes me sad to realize I've lost his friendship, maybe forever. You can't be friends with a friend once he's been your lover. I knew that, but Andy thought if we were lovers, just once, it would convince me I truly loved him." She looked at him, hoping he understood. Although he was watching her closely, she sensed a certain tension in him that she couldn't quite define.

"But it didn't work?" Josh asked.

When Amy shook her head, she could feel her heavy curls against her cheeks. She reached up and pulled all her hair forward over one shoulder. "I just felt hollow," she said. "And I knew it was wrong. I hurt him so badly, Josh. I'm surprised he doesn't hate me."

"How do you know he doesn't?"

She gazed at him intently, sensing the faint tension again. A flash of insight left her cold. "You would hate me, wouldn't you?"

He laughed. "I might. But you didn't feel hollow with me, did you?"

A heated blush rose swiftly up her throat, and she lifted her chin. "I wouldn't have made love with you the second time if I did."

His lips parted in a half smile. "Close call for me."

She wondered just what he meant, and then leaned back on the bed to snuggle beside him under the quilt. He reached an arm under her head and kissed her hair.

"So Andy was your first?" he asked.

"No," she said, and by the way his fingers stopped stroking her hair, she guessed she'd surprised him. "I had a boyfriend in college, but that didn't last long."

"Why? What happened?"

She shrugged. "I wasn't intense enough for him. I didn't have enough angst. He dumped me."

"*He* dumped *you?*"

She laughed. "You sound so shocked."

"I am."

She had been, too, at first. In fact, the sting had been intolerable at the time, and the insult, too. In the end, she had found it bitterly ironic that Brad had said she wasn't intense enough, and then she'd suffered intensely after he dumped her. Her first attempt at love had taught her not to want to inflict that kind of pain on anyone else if she could help it, so she'd felt even worse when she broke Andy's heart. Altogether, her experiences had convinced her to keep men at arm's length, and it had been easy enough to do with the dozen or so friendly guys she'd had in her life. Or at least, it had been easy until Josh. She was already dangling by one hand over a new pit of intensity, and heaven knew how she was going to get out alive.

"Now you know all my dark secrets," she said.

"No," he said quietly. "Not all of them."

She turned in his arms to see his face, but it told her nothing. "What else is there?"

He touched one finger above her heart, and she felt

his cool touch like a stone falling into a pool, sending off ripples and vibrations all through the dark water.

"Why can you still run away from me?" he asked.

She shivered. "It was just one picnic, Josh."

"You know what I mean."

She didn't know, yet at the same time she felt a strange withdrawing, some deep inner flaw she'd never sensed before. Could he be right? Could she be afraid of the risk of learning to love him? She knew from now on her body was going to crave him whether she was with him or not. Didn't that prove her willingness to try to make this relationship work? Or maybe he was referring to his daughters again.

She sighed, frowning absently at the pile of books on her dresser.

"Why do I get the feeling we're having two different conversations?" she asked.

"Let me show you something," he said, turning the light off again. He lifted his hand toward the skylights, and she watched the angle of his finger as he pointed out the Big Dipper. Then he traced the handle of the pot-shaped constellation that pointed toward the last star in the tail of the Little Dipper. "Do you know what that is?" he asked.

"The North Star."

"Wrong," he said. "That's the Kita Star. It never rises and never sets. It's more powerful than the moon or the sun because it's constant."

Amy smiled in the darkness, absorbing the magical quality of his voice. She had always liked the North Star, and she could imagine how significant it had been to him growing up, knowing a star with his own name was glowing in the sky.

"So the Kita Star is you?" she asked.

"No. That's what I've been looking for."

A sinking feeling wrapped around her heart. She wasn't constant. She was a canoe guide, wild and free, untethered by any relationships that might hold her down. She wasn't *ready* to be constant, no matter how extraordinary Josh was in bed. He couldn't be asking that of her. The silence stretched out and took on a strained quality, but Amy didn't know how to answer. She couldn't see his face in the dark.

"And on that dire note . . . ," he said ironically.

"You're not going?"

He kissed her lightly and started getting up.

"I have to fly home," he said. "I don't want the girls to wake up without me there."

She sat up and watched him reach for his pants and pull them on. He put on his socks, then tied his shoes. Stay with me, she thought. At least until the sun comes up.

He glanced around the bedroom, then smiled at her. "My shirt's downstairs," he said. "Don't get up."

She didn't want to get up. She wanted him to lie down again. But she couldn't say the words because he had daughters to go home to.

He stood at her bedside and put his hands on his hips so she could see the flexed muscles of his shoulders and chest. He looked so incredible she longed to sit up and press her lips against him again, to feel his warm flesh alive and responding.

"Don't look at me that way," he said.

She put every ounce of seduction she had into her expression. "What way?"

He groaned and picked up a pillow and tossed it at her. "This is a responsible adult trying to say 'happy trails.' "

She chuckled and hugged the pillow. "All right," she said. "Sex for fun will have to wait for another trail, I guess."

He looked at her oddly for a second, and then smiled. "See you," he said, and a minute later he was gone.

Several hours later, when Amy woke up and went into the kitchen for a quick cup of coffee before work, she looked in the pot of fudge and saw that a greedy spoon-scoop had been taken out, right in the middle.

SEVEN

Dammit all to hell, he thought. Didn't she know how incredible their lovemaking was? Didn't he mean anything to her at all? He clutched the small black wheel of the seaplane and swore until he'd exhausted his vocabulary, and then he started over again.

He was almost home as the sun was breaking over the horizon, and though it was one of the most glorious sunrises he'd seen in a long time, he hardly noticed.

And Andy! Curse his wholesome, hardworking bones. It wasn't so bad that Andy had known Amy before he had. What killed Josh was that Andy had tried basically the same approach of trying to win her over through sex. So much for being original. And if the hometown sweetheart hadn't succeeded, what chance did he have?

"Well, at least I didn't make her feel hollow," he muttered out loud. "Geez!"

He brought the plane down on Blue Gill Lake and taxied over to his designated spot in the marina. Then he turned the key, slumped forward, and feeling tired, he rested his chin on top of his hands and gazed out the little windshield, peering toward the rising sun. He should be exhilarated after the best night of sex he'd experienced in years, maybe ever. He should be thrilled that he was involved with the most intoxicating, most bewitching, most irritating woman he'd ever known. Instead, he felt an intense, hungry loneliness that threatened to consume him. He wanted her so badly he ached, and yet at the same time he realized he must have known making love to her wasn't going to be enough. Why was he surprised that she hadn't even once whispered that she loved him? asked the cynic in him. Not even when she was lost in abandon, when she couldn't be held accountable for what she said, not even as a lie or as a courtesy had she said anything about love.

That was because she was honest. He took a hard look at what he had to offer her, and his lips twisted in self-derision. He wasn't that much older than she was, chronologically, but being a father put him in a completely separate category. It was almost like being from a different culture, with a different set of rules and a different language. The father role he cherished was what separated him from her most. Why should she choose to team up with someone who had already been down a marriage road, and failed, when she could unite with some untried soul and take on the adventure and build their own story, their own family, from scratch?

He swore again. What the hell was he doing, thinking about marriage with a woman who couldn't even stand to go on a picnic with his daughters? Get real, Kita. But underneath his disgust, he recognized an uglier feeling. He hurt. The one thing he'd been craving the last five years was someone to really love him and his daughters.

And Amy didn't love his daughters. He tried to be fair: She hadn't known them long, and they *had* been difficult. Obnoxious even, in Chloe's case. Amy was honest when she said she loved kids; he was certain about that. She didn't have to be a homemaker type to be a loving mother someday. He would just have to accept that there wasn't an instant bond between the three of them. He'd have to be satisfied that the potential was there.

He groaned out loud and prayed he wasn't deceiving himself. If Amy couldn't learn to love him *and* his girls, then he'd only be torturing himself as long as he let his infatuation continue. He let out a savage laugh. Infatuation nothing. He had a mental image of her delicate, warm hair wrapped in his fingers, and groaned. He was already more captivated by Amy's wanton sweetness than he had ever been ensnared by all of Shannon's manipulations. He might have cornered Amy once in her kitchen, but she had him where it counted.

"There's a call for you, Amy," Larry yelled from the office steps. "He said he'll hold until you get over here."

In front of Dinah's Depot, Amy was helping to move a table to a shaded area, but she looked in Larry's direction and felt a tremor of anticipation go through her. She received a dozen calls every day, but from the butterflies in her gut, she already knew it had to be Josh. She'd missed him when he called earlier that week, and had reached only his machine when she tried back.

"Go on," Dinah said. "I've got this under control."

As she hurried toward the office, Amy felt a surge of restless anxiety, knowing the success of Home Trail Outfitters was almost as vital to Dinah as it was to Rex. Rex, Amy noticed, was in the canoe repair shop, a sure sign that he was anxious, too, since he rarely worked in the shop during the day.

As she breezed into the office, she noticed it was momentarily empty, and she hurried to the back room and picked up the receiver.

"Amy here," she said.

"It's me, Josh."

A flood of relief and pleasure coursed through her, and she pivoted slightly toward the wall so she could talk without Larry hearing her. In the spacious back room where there were several tables and desks, two other staff members were pouring over a map, their voices muted in the background.

"What's up?" she asked.

"What did you ever do with that paper boat I gave you? I didn't see it at your house."

The intimate, friendly tone of his voice took her miles away from where she stood, and she closed her eyes to feel even closer to him. "It's in the living room. On the mantel," she said. "How did you like the fudge?"

"I should have taken the whole pot. I want the recipe."

She smiled into the receiver and opened her eyes again. "You'll have to get it from my mother."

"When can I meet her?"

An odd sensation floated in her belly, and she stared hard at her fingernails. Her cuticles needed to be pushed back. "She doesn't usually fly over from Dublin to give out recipes."

"Would she if I asked her to?"

She just might, Amy thought. "Now you're being absurd."

"Let's just say," he began, "that my mother would be dying of curiosity to meet you if she hadn't met you already."

"Not all mothers are equally curious."

"They are when their adult children are out all night long. Besides, I'd like to meet your mother."

"I got that already. Is that why you called?"

Josh laughed. "I want you to sign us up for a canoe trip, me and the girls. One that you're leading."

Pure energy hammered around her lungs and robbed her of breath. "I'm sorry," she said. "We're completely booked until late August. I wish you'd told me sooner."

"I didn't know you sooner. Can't you fit us in?"

She jammed her hand down into her shorts pocket. Her mind raced over a series of unrelated thoughts: Josh and his daughters would be her responsibility. He looked like a god in her bed. She couldn't possibly be in a canoe with him. "How long a trip were you thinking of?"

"An overnight?"

She moved toward the calendar and scanned the blocks of July, each about three inches square and jammed full of trip numbers. Adding three people would mean adding a full canoe load, and most of the one-night trips were already filled to the four-canoe capacity. She frowned at a number and set her finger on a trip marked in purple ink while she scanned through another book.

"Are you serious about this?" she asked.

"Do you have something?"

"Well, I don't know if you'll be interested," she said. "I have one trip scheduled in two weeks that's been booked by a music camp, five teenagers and their counselor."

"What are they, a chorus or something?" Josh asked.

"Sometimes. It's different every year. They called to cut their numbers last week, and their counselor told me it would be all right to combine them with another trip."

"There's no chance just you and I and the girls can take a trip together?"

She laughed at the pleading tone in his voice, scanning her eyes over the busy calendar. "Not unless you want to try September. The phone's been ringing off the hook. I guess the advertising has paid off and the word of mouth hasn't hurt any, either. Rex should have his best year ever, and then some."

"He should be happy."

Amy thought so too. But Rex, who had emerged from the repair shop, was gazing at the lake, looking anything but happy. Watching him through the window, Amy felt a shiver of fear, as if she'd missed something, forgotten something important.

"How are Chloe and Hannah?" Amy asked absently.

"Hannah's good. Chloe's, well, not so good."

Amy instantly forgot Rex and concentrated on Josh's voice. "What do you mean?"

"Chloe's having more trouble," he said. She could hear the fatigue and concern in his voice; he almost sounded like a different person. "She's keeping herself together better at school, but when she gets home, she falls apart. Yesterday she got so mad she took off her glasses and threw them across the room."

"Oh, no," she said, feeling a twinge of guilt, as if she herself were somehow responsible. "What did you do?"

"I told her to go up to her room and calm down. What else could I do?"

Amy didn't know. "Was she okay?"

"She pulled out of it. My parents came over for dinner and she brightened a little. I don't know, Amy. She's having a hard time. I had a talk with the school psychiatrist about her, and she said this sort of behavior isn't unusual, considering. She said it was a good sign that Chloe could keep it together at school, and that she must feel safe falling apart at home. She recommended we try a couple of therapy sessions and see if it helps. I don't know."

His simple expression of doubt spoke volumes for how worried he was, and Amy wished she could help out somehow.

"Do you think the canoe trip's a good idea?" she asked.

Josh didn't answer immediately. "I wouldn't suggest it if I didn't think so."

"I'm sorry."

She stood waiting, feeling the receiver get heavier and heavier in her hand.

"Look," he said. "I know some people might think I shouldn't even be considering a relationship with you with everything that's going on. Hell, I can argue myself that my first obligation is to my daughters. But I'm not abandoning Chloe and Hannah if I want to see you sometimes too."

"On the other hand, Chloe just tried to ruin her own glasses." She bit on the inside of her cheek until it stung. "Perhaps her logic isn't at its strongest."

Amy winced, expecting an explosion from his end of the phone. Instead, she heard a sharp rapping noise, as if he'd just started tapping a pencil against the edge of a desk. If they were going to try to have a real relationship, she would have to tell him what she thought, even if it wasn't always comfortable. The silence lasted so long she began to hope he wasn't really mad, but at the first sound of his voice she knew he was furious.

"Fine," he said. "When's the open weekend? Two weeks from now? Sign us up. We'll see you then."

While he didn't exactly hang up on her, it was a darn good imitation.

Her last exchange with Josh gnawed at her until she couldn't tell anymore if she'd imagined the tension or not. If he was really mad, he'd call to clear it up with her, she reasoned. And if he wasn't mad and she called him to find out if he was, then she'd be making a big deal out of nothing. Dead silence went totally against her nature, so she finally tried to reach him. When she got his answering machine instead, her words tripped out with annoying vacuity. He left a polite reply on her machine but made no suggestion that they try to get together again before the canoe trip. She listened to it four times, trying to glean information from the tone of his voice, then erased it in frustration. He was getting to her. He'd probably timed the call on purpose for when she wouldn't be home. If she called back *another* time, would she seem desperate?

Maybe he was focused on spending time with his daughters.

Then again, maybe he was trying to teach her what it was like not to have him in her life.

Every time she went to work she half expected to find he'd canceled his trip, but his name remained on the list, and his deposit was on file. The message light on her answering machine at home refused to blink.

"He's playing mind games with you," Cottie said, when she'd cornered Amy outside the post office, trying to pry out significant details.

Amy shook her head. "I don't think so."

"You don't *think* so," Cottie echoed, as if Amy had just proven her point. "That's mind-game talk. He's a wily one. Has he made love to you yet?"

"Cottie!" Amy rubbernecked the area in front of the post office to make sure nobody could overhear her sister-in-law.

"I knew it!" Cottie squealed. "Madge is going to be thrilled!"

"You aren't going to tell Madge. What kind of sister are you?"

Cottie giggled and held up her pile of letters to point them at her. "All right," she said. "Of course I won't. But I can't wait to see you all fixed up. What are his daughters like?"

Amy hesitated, then decided it wasn't breach of confidence if she told Cottie that Josh's oldest daughter was having a little trouble adjusting to losing her mother. Cottie's auburn eyebrows arched sympathetically over her blue eyes, and her hand curled protectively over her protruding stomach.

"That poor girl," she said. "I can't imagine how awful that would be. She must feel like she has no balance left at all in her life."

Amy suddenly felt off kilter as if Cottie's words had temporarily robbed her of her own balance. The feeling resonated with an old memory, a feeling she'd had after her father died. She glanced along the main street of Harmony, seeing the familiar shops, the geraniums, and the video store. In the warm, late afternoon light, a blue bike was parked outside the hardware store, and a dog was sniffing at a lamppost. Shoppers were going into and out of the IGA, pushing grocery carts empty and full.

She remembered biking along this same street once when her father was ill, and even though she had known the main street wouldn't change once he was dead, she had tried to memorize exactly how it looked so she'd always remember how she felt when her father was alive. Later, when he died, the street did look different to her, the distances shorter, the buildings narrower, the curbs lower, as if she had been suddenly swept forward beyond all her child-size perceptions.

She had seriously doubted what the point of life was, and she hadn't trusted that other people she loved would stay healthy and live. Intellectually, she knew she wasn't being reasonable, but emotionally, she didn't count on the future.

Was that how Chloe was feeling? Amy wondered. Like she couldn't count on anything? And what about the way Briana and Lee's wedding had disturbed Amy? *They* believed in a future; *they* were trusting in love. Even Amy's own mother, and Nigel. And Cottie and Sean. They all believed they'd have full lives together. The disconnected ideas swirled through her mind, confusing her.

"You all right?" Cottie asked, putting her hand on Amy's arm.

"Yes," she said. "I'm just thinking."

"Why don't you come have dinner with us? Sean wants to see you."

"I can't," Amy said. "I have too much work. In a couple of weeks, maybe." By then the canoe trip with Josh would be over.

Chloe. Amy's father. Josh. They were all connected somehow. Amy just had to figure out the links, and she had a feeling she was going to have to look inward before she could find any answers outside herself.

The morning of July twelfth dawned warm and windless, with a forecast of late afternoon showers and evening temperatures in the fifties. Amy was already at the outfitters helping to load canoes on the trailer and to pack food rations and camping gear. There were four Duluth packs: one for food; three for tents, cooking pots, and personal gear. She counted ten personal floatation devices, or PFDs as they called them, and eight paddles. All of Rex's staff was setting up for other trips—every canoe they owned would be on the water this weekend, and the festive activity of the packing area filled her heart with pleasure.

How her father would have enjoyed this scene. It was almost like a departure morning from voyageur days, 150 years before. Back then, there would have been shouted French and laughter, calico and buckskin, colorful knit caps and brawny arms, beards and knives and jaunty posing, while now there were bright nylon PFDs and baseball caps, sweet-smelling sunscreen, and dehydrated food. But the water was the same, as was the underlying current of excitement. She was proud that the blood of voyageurs ran in her veins, and that her ancestors had been among the first Minnesota pioneers.

Amy was putting her map and compass in a plastic case when the van from the music camp pulled into the lot. Almost immediately behind it, Josh's station wagon circled into view.

Walsh Harrison, a celebrated trumpet player from the Twin Cities, opened the van door and gave Amy a desperate grin. She felt her heart lighten at the sight of him and knew from experience she was going to spend the whole trip laughing at his wry humor. Walsh was followed by five teenagers—two girls and three boys— who, by their attentive politeness, looked as if they knew a lot more about recital halls than they did about canoes.

"Hi, Walsh," Amy called.

"Hey, Aim," he said. "Thank God, it's you. What do you say we elope and leave these kids in the musk egg?" He gave her a chummy kiss on the cheek, his dark beard bristling her sensitive skin. The teenage girls pointed and whispered excitedly to one another.

Amy grinned and gave him a good-natured shove. "I have a manly job to do," she said. "And you've got all the signs of a duffer."

"Look," he said, swinging a thumb toward the teenagers. "I brought the dwarves with me. Jason, Spud, Monica, Suzi, and Homer."

The kids laughed and came forward to shake hands. They were all classical musicians, two violinists, two cellists, and a percussionist, and they were burned out from practicing six hours a day at their intense music camp. An overnight in the wild was intended to refresh them so they could bring new perspective to their studies during the rest of their music camp stay. Amy put them to work packing their gear, then graced Walsh with another smile. Over the past four years, she'd enjoyed seeing him with music campers, and she couldn't help admiring him. Not many world-class trumpet players would work for peanuts to inspire a bunch of high school students.

Walsh looked over her shoulder, and Amy turned to see Josh, Chloe, and Hannah standing on the other side of the van.

"Here's the rest of our group," Amy said. "Let me introduce you."

Josh and Walsh shook hands, the girls said hello, and the musicians waved briefly. Chloe and Hannah had matching pairs of binoculars, small, colorful ones with straps to go around their necks, and Amy guessed they were gifts for the trip. Hannah held hers up to be admired, and Amy gave her a quick hug.

"Hi, sport," Amy said to Chloe, with her arm still around Hannah. "Nice to see you. Are you going to look for birds?"

"Yep," said Chloe. "And stars."

Amy smiled and couldn't resist ruffling the girl's dark blond hair. "I can show you lots of constellations. My dad taught me all about them."

She glanced up at Josh and felt a tug of attraction and anxiety. It was the first time she'd seen him in two weeks, with nothing more than the awkward phone messages, and she wished she could say more to him than a simple hello. He looked relaxed and competent, his gaze steady and thoughtful as he followed her movements.

"It's nice to see you." Her quiet voice had none of the jocularity she'd used with Walsh and the others.

He scrutinized her intimately for an instant, then smiled. "Likewise."

Amy felt her heart expand with relief. Later, she thought. They would talk later.

Like the other guides, Amy led her group through an orientation that included brief lessons on the *C* and *J* canoe strokes, what to do if a canoe swamped, how to sit and move in a canoe, safety gear, and mapping their route. After a last pause for the restrooms, sunscreen, and bug repellent, and final paperwork for Walsh and Josh, the ten of them loaded into a van with Rex, who drove them to their launch site and helped unload the canoes from the trailer.

It seemed like a lot of preparation, but once they were on the water, it was all worth it. Amy could sense the collective exhilaration as everyone realized they were off. Whooping Lake, a long, narrow lake bordered by pines on gentle slopes, was a perfect starting point because it was both breathtakingly beautiful and shaped to encourage beginners as they proceeded gradually toward the far end. Voices carried easily over the water as the more expert canoers teased or offered advice to the novices.

Amy watched Walsh's group closely at first, but soon she let them move ahead, three in each canoe, while she and Josh brought up the last two canoes. She sat in the stern of one, with Hannah in her bow, and Josh sat in the stern of the other, with Chloe ahead of him. Hannah paddled gamely at first, but her little arms tired shortly, and Amy didn't mind when the girl only occasionally dipped her paddle in the iron-rich water.

As Amy's paddle cleaved neatly into the cool water, and her wrist turned effortlessly to clear the paddle out, her muscles warmed with pleasure. She pressed her knees against the gunnels, the upper edges of the canoe's sides, to steady her body in the balanced canoe.

She looked across to Josh and heard him softly encourage Chloe to lengthen her stroke. The girl paused to push her glasses back up her nose, then drove her paddle in again. Amy was privately impressed with the girl's determination and her attentiveness. Her narrow knees poked up in view above the gunnels, and her slender back was straight when she reached her paddle forward. When Amy glanced back at Josh, a bolt of recognition ran through her.

They had the same rhythm. She and Josh, in separate canoes, were paddling at exactly the same pace. He was watching her, his smile quizzical, while their canoes moved in parallel over the blue, reflecting water. When she stopped for a moment to rest her paddle atop her knees, he stopped too, and called to Chloe to stop. As if tied to each other with invisible ropes, their canoes glided silently together, and the sun reflected tiny drops of light from their gleaming paddles to make trails in the water.

"Wow," she said.

"You're good at this," Josh said. "This makes sense, to see you here."

"I'd better be good at it. I've been doing it all my life."

She'd never experienced quite this sort of happiness on a canoe trip before. Then she did what she'd been longing to do for two weeks. She drank in the sight of him: his dark, wind-tossed hair; his faintly exotic eyes; the elegant, ironic line of his lips. His jaw was proud and bold, his tan neck strong and angled with masculine grace. His rugged shoulders were outlined clearly beneath his black shirt, and the short sleeves showed biceps and forearms that were flexed with toned muscle and restrained strength. Every inch of him was magnetically appealing, and the effect on her was so powerful she could swear her canoe was being drawn closer to his across the water. She felt suddenly thirsty and had to lick her lips, which caused his gaze to shoot to her mouth. When he looked back up to meet her eyes, she could see a half-starved expression in his face that made her want to groan.

Josh mentally cursed. If he'd thought it was bad living without her for two weeks, living in close quarters with her for forty-eight hours without being able to touch her was going to be hell.

And Walsh. If Walsh was typical of the friendly guys Amy liked to hang out with, it was a miracle she hadn't been scooped up long before. It had taken him a cool thirty seconds to assess the man and to see there was absolutely zero chemistry between them, at least on Amy's side. Josh had felt a surge of masculine possessiveness and pleasure when he realized he had no cause for jealousy. At the same time, it annoyed him that Walsh knew things about Amy that he didn't, and that was something he intended to rectify.

"Walsh calls you Aim," Josh said, as they began paddling again.

"My real name's Amelia. Most people call me Amy, but my family and a few of my friends call me Aim sometimes."

"I like it."

"What's your middle name?" she asked.

"I don't have one. It's just Joshua Kita." He shrugged. "What's yours?"

"Amelia Gladys Larkspur. After my two grand-mothers."

"I'm named after my grandmother," Chloe said.

"I'm named after a dog," Hannah said.

Josh laughed. "You are not."

"Yes, I am," Hannah said, and went into a story about a dog that lived next door to them in California. It took her father a while to dislodge the misinformation from Hannah's memory, and in the meantime, the girls ran through a series of California stories in embarrassing detail. Though Amy asked no questions, he could see her storing up the clues: Chloe's birthday when Shannon sent a surprise clown because she couldn't be there herself; the videotape of the preschool holiday show they made for Shannon and how they watched it later with popcorn; the handmade Halloween costumes Josh made using a stapler to secure the seams.

His oldest daughter seemed so happy remembering those days that he was reluctant to distract her, but he knew from watching Amy's absent smile that she was hearing the real story between the staples and videos. Chloe finally slowed down.

"And then we moved to New York with Mom," she said. "And Daddy stayed behind."

"And there was another dog named Hannah there too," said Hannah.

Josh laughed around the pain in his heart, and pulled harder on the canoe paddle, unintentionally sending his canoe ahead of Amy's.

"Should we catch up with the others?" he asked.

He had hoped the canoe trip would give his daughters a chance to get to know Amy better, but throughout the rest of the day, he noticed something else happening. Time and again, over trail lunch, after a swim, and when collecting firewood, Chloe would tell old stories from their life before the divorce. Chloe had been going on four, Hannah going on two, hardly old enough to remember, or so he'd thought. Even Hannah recalled surprising details when prompted.

Josh couldn't see why they were parading these memories before Amy, unless it somehow comforted them to review their early childhoods when they felt loved by both their parents. He could see Amy on the fringe, listening, even as she gave instructions to the other campers, helped set up the three tents, and started dinner over a campfire. Yet he couldn't guess what she thought about his daughters, and there was no way to ask.

As dinner ended, clouds began to gather overhead, bringing the darkness prematurely. Amy briefed everyone on what to do if the lightning became extreme, but their campsite was not exposed, and the forecast had been for showers, not thunderstorms. When the rain came, the drops were so sudden and fat that the girls ran gleefully for their tent. Josh went with Amy to help roll over the canoes on the shore, their bottoms up toward the rain, with the PFDs and paddles stored beneath. Walsh was busy suspending the food pack between two trees to keep it safe from bears and raccoons. The rain was falling so loudly and heavily Josh could barely see through it, but Amy only laughed, hurrying to help Walsh.

"Go look after the girls," Amy yelled.

"What else needs to be done?" Josh asked, calling through the rain.

"This is it. Go on. I'll join you in a minute."

Amy roped the last knots with Walsh and felt rain

hit her face as she looked up at the big green Duluth pack slung between the trees. A flash of lightning shot the whole area with an instant of blue light.

"Come play charades with us," Walsh called over the thunder.

Amy squinted through the rain at the three tents lined around the campsite. The middle tent was slightly larger, and all the musicians were in there now. The tent for Josh's family was smaller, and two pale circles of light from flashlights inside were visible through the sloping sides.

Amy grinned at Walsh. "Not a chance."

"Just as I thought. I never had good timing with anything but music." Walsh hurried into the middle tent and was greeted by laughter.

Amy hurried to Josh's tent and unzipped the door. "Let me in, let me in!"

Lightning flashed behind her as she came in and zipped the door closed again. Each girl was huddled on a sleeping bag, holding a flashlight, and they looked nervous with their big eyes and little mouths. Josh was bare-chested behind them, and Amy realized she'd interrupted him changing into a dry shirt.

"Oh! I'm sorry," she said. "I can go—"

"No!" Both girls instantly reached for her and held on to her arms.

Though she averted her face from Josh and concentrated on Hannah's round eyes, she was keenly aware that just beyond her view he was putting on a dry shirt, and he wasn't hurrying, either.

"You aren't afraid of a little thunder, are you?" she asked.

"No," Hannah said, but the next crack made her jump.

Amy laughed. "Let me tell you about real thunder." She launched into a story of another night when the storm was so bad she and her friends had left their tent, which was exposed, up on a granite rock and sat on their life jackets, scattered in a row in the forest, counting off by number after each crack of thunder to be sure they were all still okay.

"Are you serious?" Josh asked.

Amy nodded, looking over to see him in a green chamois shirt with two pockets on the chest. In the dim interior of the tent, the color was almost black, the texture inviting.

"She's joking," Chloe said.

"No, I'm not," she said. "It's safer that way. If we all stayed in one tent, and the tent was hit—*bam!* That would be it. And the ground current is as bad as the lightning."

Chloe looked nervously at the angling roof of the tent. "Should we go out?" she asked.

Amy laughed again and spoke in her most reassuring voice. "No. This is a perfectly safe spot, and listen, the thunder's going away already."

The girls' expressions showed concern as they listened closely, and the rain was so loud around them, it drowned out all other sound. Suddenly a flash of lightning blasted around them, the thunder banging at the same instant, and Hannah screamed. She bolted upward and threw her arms around the closest person: her older sister. Though Chloe looked none too sanguine herself, she put her hand over Hannah's eyes and held her close.

"It's okay, Hannah," Chloe said.

Hannah clutched her big sister even harder and kept her face huddled against Chloe's chest. When Josh shifted closer to both girls, Chloe sat up a little straighter and shook her head slightly. "I've got her," she said.

Amy saw Josh's surprise, but then he relaxed. The last big clap of thunder was followed only by weaker bangs, and they listened to the receding rumbles as the rain continued to rush down around the tent. Hannah slumped against Chloe, and after another few moments, Chloe put her glasses into her shoe and both girls snuggled down in the sleeping bags, right up against each other, their heads on one pillow.

Josh propped one flashlight up so it shone against the corner angle of the roof, casting just enough light to make the interior cozy, but not enough to disturb sleep.

Amy was just about to leave when Chloe sat up again and squinted at her. "Will you be nearby?" she asked.

Amy felt a twist go through her heart, and she leaned forward and gently smoothed Chloe's hair back behind her ear. Without her glasses, the girl had a large-eyed, fragile beauty that was haunting in the shadowy dimness, and Amy was strangely moved by a longing she couldn't identify.

"I'll be near," she said softly. "I'm sleeping with Monica and Suzi, right in the other tent. Listen, you can hear their voices."

Sure enough, as the rain had diminished to an occasional drop, they could hear soft laughter from the other tents, and someone was singing a low ballad. Chloe smiled as she lay back down.

"Good night," Chloe said.

Amy leaned near and gave her a quick kiss on the

forehead. "Good night, precious." She gave Hannah a kiss too. "Sweet dreams."

"That's what Mom used to say," Chloe murmured, but her tone was merely contemplative, without any challenge or sadness in it. "Sweet dreams, Amy."

She felt a thickness in her throat and swallowed hard, avoiding Josh's gaze. She backed out of the tent and stood for a moment, trying to clear her head and get her bearings in the new darkness. The storm had left pockets of stars in the sky and a fresh dampness that made everything smell green and wild in the darkness. A glance at the other tents showed her there were lights in both, so the girls, Monica and Suzi, had retired to their own tent, while Walsh and the three boys had apparently started a poker game in the larger one. She shivered, but she couldn't bear the idea of going into one of the tents while her mind was still whirling. She wanted to think about Chloe, Hannah, and Josh, and why they made her feel so utterly helpless and emotional, all of them. All Chloe did was wish her sweet dreams, and her heart was a yo-yo.

Wrapping her arms around her, she stepped gingerly through the darkness toward the granite of the shoreline, seeking solitude. After pulling a dry PFD from under a canoe, she found a sheltered area on the shore a little way from the campsite and sat down on the makeshift cushion. A sylvan breeze hushed in the balsam, tamarack, and spruce trees behind her, shaking loose a patter of drops before it stilled again. Clouds continued to scuttle across the night sky, but in the east the clouds had moonlight halos that glowed eerily and sent a film of luminescence over the lake. It was so beautiful, so solitary, her heart went raw with inexplicable pain. Again she shivered, wishing she'd grabbed a sweater, and then, preparing to face the emotional confusion that rocked her heart, she buried her face against her knees.

A calm male voice came out of the darkness.

"Is this seat taken?"

EIGHT

When Josh saw her look over her shoulder and lift her moist brown eyes to his, every water molecule that was suspended in the cool, damp air suddenly aligned its charges, lacing the space between them with precision electricity. He could feel it in each hair on his neck and in the breath in his lungs and in the raw hunger that pushed to the surface of his heart. Damn, he thought, he could do nothing to control the effect she had on him.

"How did you find me?" she asked.

"I tracked you."

He spread out a tarp beside her, the plastic crinkling over the long, wet grass, and then he spread out his sleeping bag to sit on. Very subtle, Kita, he mentally groaned. But when he reached for her she shifted off her life vest cushion and joined him on the sleeping bag, settling against his chest. He ran his palms down her sleeves and felt her shiver.

"Cold?" he asked.

"A little."

He'd put a sweatshirt over his chamois shirt; he pulled it off and wrapped her up in it. Now when he nestled his nose against her shoulder and neck, she smelled like his own clean laundry, and the scent was oddly erotic. As if he needed more stimulation.

"Better?"

She nodded. "Oh, Josh," she said, putting her arms around his neck. "I missed you."

He felt a savage triumph grind through him. Their time apart was not a lot of time in the whole scheme of things, but long enough for him to see if she noticed at all.

"That's only fair," he said.

He hugged her hard, sliding her onto his lap, and he closed his eyes at the sweet pressure of her chest against his. When he gazed down again, her face was very near in the dimness, and he could see the shadowy gap of her lips inviting him to kiss her.

"Where are the mosquitoes?" he asked.

"The rain and the cold have slowed them down, for now."

"Are all the campers in their tents?"

"They were when I left."

"The girls were sleeping," Josh said. "I asked Walsh to keep an ear out for them."

He took one of her hands in his and smoothed her long fingers with his thumb. How could she be so delicate and so strong at the same time? Something powerful had happened back there in the tent when Amy leaned over to give his daughters good-night kisses. They were too young to go to bed every night without a mother, and Amy would be a great mom if she'd let herself. He turned his mind away from the idea, unwilling to let himself dream too far. It had to be enough that she was there with him, letting him hold her.

"Did you see Chloe with Hannah?" she asked, her voice hardly more than a whisper in the moonlight.

He nodded, watching her closely. "I think tonight was a sort of breakthrough for her," he said. Though he didn't know how to describe what it had been like, seeing the girls bonding so closely with each other, he'd felt a pang of exclusion. It was an ache he had felt long ago when he was left out of the girls' life because of the divorce. Remembering it now, he knew the comfort that Hannah and Chloe had given each other was a quiet tribute to growth and survival, and he knew, ultimately, that the sibling closeness would never diminish his importance as their father. He exhaled slowly and drew Amy closer.

"They're growing so fast," he said. "It really amazes me. Even in the three months they've been with me, they've changed so much."

"You're a good father."

Her compliment meant a lot to him. The love he felt for Chloe and Hannah was fierce and complex, full of past disappointments and hopes for future closeness. They would always be the most important focus of his life.

Yet at the same time, he knew that another side of him was incomplete. It was like having an iron mine with two shafts in it, a rich one and an empty one; even though all the activity and energy were devoted to the full shaft, he couldn't forget that the other shaft of unfulfilled promise still branched off into underground darkness.

He wanted Amy, and he wasn't complete without her. He wanted her so badly it was annoying. As a logical person, he knew there should be a way to make her love him, but to do so he needed to be able to think clearly, and he couldn't think clearly because he was already half-lost to being in love with her. This was what annoyed him, because he didn't believe he could honestly fall in love with a person who wasn't in love with him.

So, either she *did* love him back and just wasn't saying so, or he wasn't honestly falling in love with her.

He grit his teeth. "I'm having conversations in my head."

"What about?"

"Love theorems," he said, and he could feel she was startled. He plunged on. "There's love," he said, "and there's the illusion of love."

"This, I've got to hear. Expert."

"I'm no expert."

"Let's hear it anyway," she said.

"The illusion of love," he began, "has identifiable symptoms: shortness of breath in the presence of the love object, muddled thinking, and increased energy level and productivity."

She chuckled and shifted against him, resting her cheek on his shoulder. From across the lake, a loon called into the night.

"How is that different from real love?" she asked.

"Real love also has shortness of breath, muddled thinking, and increased energy."

"So, what's the difference?" she asked.

"Real love happens to both people simultaneously. The illusion of love can happen to one person alone, and it has a nasty crash factor."

He could feel her holding herself very still. He tried

to keep his arms relaxed around her, but every muscle was tense with apprehension.

"Are you trying to tell me something?" she asked.

"See if you can guess."

Oh, good God, she thought, here it was.

She had never been good at guessing games, but when she felt his kiss on her neck and felt the strong urgency in his arms as he embraced her, she knew, as far as she was concerned, the game was hopelessly lost. She ran her fingers over the soft chamois of his shirt, loving the texture and the heat of his skin beneath. As she inhaled deeply, the intoxicating scent of the lush, damp pine needles was inextricably woven into her sensory intake of Josh. He was like a prince of the forest, a god of the lake, power and endurance, and the throbbing pulse of life itself.

As his hands carressed her under the heavy cotton of the sweatshirt he'd loaned her, she shivered, but not from cold. As Josh eased her back onto the sleeping bag and tarp, the temperature seemed to rise ten degrees. She knew full well he had planned this, that she was playing right into his seduction, but if he hadn't come out to join her by the lake, she would have died of unfilled need by the time she went back to the campsite.

With tantalizing patience, his fingers found the front clasp of her bra under her two layers of clothing, and her breasts welcomed the release. She stretched along the sleeping bag, silently urging him to roll his weight onto hers, and when he did, his strong legs were heavy and muscular above her own. Through his trousers, the hard center of his loins pressed against her pelvis with intimate familiarity, and she instinctively sucked her breath upward to create a matching convex heat in the muscles of her lower abdomen. Half-propped on his elbows to keep from crushing her, he kissed her cheeks and eyelids, then finally her lips again, while she felt each new sensation in a dazzled haze. She locked her fingers behind his neck and arched to press her body against his and kiss him. With a groan he crushed her into the circle of his arms, allowing her only enough room to inhale.

"My God, you're sweet," he said.

She couldn't resist a reply. "As sweet as wet clothes can make me."

She saw the pale gleam of his teeth as he grinned, and then he was kissing behind her ear.

"All right then. Better than a marshmallow," he said.

"Raw or burned?"

"Would you just kiss me?" he demanded.

She was happy to oblige him. Amy had never made love with so many clothes on before, and while the fabric hampered her need to feel his skin, it made the scant inches of skin she could reach all the more incredible to touch. She slid her fingers down his back and beneath the waistband of his trousers, and heard him suck in his breath. When she slid her fingers around his waist toward the buckle of his belt, his lips stilled against her throat, and she knew he was losing his concentration to the sensations that were coursing through him. The understanding brought her keen pleasure and a sense of power, and with wicked curiosity, she began an experiment. Trailing her fingers up his back, away from his waist, she found he began to kiss her again, but as she drew her fingers back to his waist and slowly unbuckled his belt, his lips slowed and his breathing grew more shallow.

She shifted beneath him so that he rolled to his

back, and then she began an earnest exploration of his torso, spanning her fingers along his chest under the warm chamois of his shirt, then following planes of muscle and the angle of hair that descended beneath his trousers. When Josh tried to pull her close against him, she evaded his hands and stroked him more confidently, knowing he was letting her tease him. As she could feel the pleasure building in his body, the anticipation in her own body began to escalate unbearably, until she had to give in when he tried again to pull her near.

"Oh, God, Amy."

With unsteady hands, he undid the top of her jeans and worked them down her legs. For an instant he sat up, and only the sweatshirt provided her with some protection against the cold. Then his naked thighs came against her with a shock, and the pressure of his arousal was hot and hard against her intimate folds. She arched toward him, wordlessly urging him on, and with heart-stopping swiftness he drove into her, filling her to a bursting point of no return. With all her strength she held on to her edge of control, but the pleasure building inside her was stronger than she was and with a moan she gave herself to the rhythm that consumed her, that consumed them both.

If the lake had risen and swept over her, she wouldn't have noticed. If the heavens had parted and a second storm had erupted around them, she couldn't have cared. She was lost in a world where there was only Josh and the exquisite feelings that radiated through her body. She spun with him, beyond gravity and light, out to where the stars twirled and exploded, and then the cosmic waves took over, one pulsing jolt of sensation after the other, a rush of ecstasy more brilliant than anything she'd ever known.

She gasped out his name, and with one final thrust he shuddered against her, clutching her hard against his heart. With her eyes clenched tightly and her breath still coming in sharp gasps, she felt the last ripples of their intimacy tremble through her, leaving her hopelessly, permanently changed.

She had been denying something, she realized. She had been afraid to fully acknowledge what this meant to her. There were promises that could be made without words, promises all the more powerful because they were forged in a language of ambiguous trust. In her unconscious efforts to protect herself earlier, she hadn't seen this, hadn't felt it deep in the raw core of her. But as she lay in his arms and heard the gentle lapping of the lake below, there was a new truth in her life that was as solid as the earth beneath them, as magical as the wash of stars that competed with the moon to illuminate the sky.

"Tell me it isn't an illusion," Josh said finally.

"No," she whispered. "It's real." And her heart swelled with the truth of it: She loved him. She loved him as she'd never loved anyone in her whole life. She thought the discovery ought to terrify her; it would have terrified the Amy who'd existed an hour ago. But she had inexplicably changed, and the proof of it showed in the marvel she felt.

She, Amy Larkspur, loved Josh Kita.

"Ouch!" Josh swore. "The mosquitoes showed up."

Amy chuckled and sat up to arrange her clothes. "There are hazards to this."

"This is ridiculous, you know," he said. "We're two grown adults sneaking around like campers playing hooky."

"I'm glad nobody else is prowling around."

"I have a feeling Walsh knows what's going on."

"Walsh?"

"He has Former Friendly Guy written all over him."

"I don't know what you mean," she said.

He laughed. "I know." He touched her chin and kissed her lips. "Adorable."

She stood up with him and brushed off her clothes. Her knees felt funny, kind of wobbly, and she knew what from. She smiled in the dark, promising herself she'd remember every moment of this stolen night. Josh smacked at his neck and rolled his tarp and bag with impressive speed.

"We have things to talk about," he said.

"Like what?"

"Like tomorrow."

"Tomorrow? We canoe to our pick-up site."

He gave her shoulder a quick squeeze. "Very funny." Then he stepped aside to let her precede him up the shore to their campsite, and she picked up her PFD, frowning.

"You think everything's funny," she said.

"I'm more serious than I've ever been."

"We're having two different conversations again."

"No, we're not."

She laughed, increasingly confused.

He paused to give her a last kiss, a warm, gentle kiss that rocked her all the way through to her toes. "Same conversation," he said decisively. "You just haven't realized it yet."

In the canoe next to Amy's, Monica was checking her tan lines, arching around in her bikini in an effort to see her own shoulder. Suzi, from the stern of Monica's canoe, said something Amy couldn't hear and both of them dissolved into laughter, causing one of the boys to yell out a joke about manly women. Monica angled her paddle to splash water at the other canoe, and the boys laughed even more.

Amy could sense the camaraderie among all the canoers, and she knew she'd be sorry to see this particular canoe trip come to an end. Through having breakfast, breaking camp, and paddling of the first lakes of the morning, there had been constant, lighthearted ribbing, some of it directed at her and Josh. Somehow, the teenagers had picked up on the chemistry between her and Josh, and with caustic looks at Walsh, they whistled the opening notes of a tune that she recognized as "The Gypsy Rover." In the convoluted code language of teenagers, they were clearly designating Walsh as a loser. The tallest boy picked up the tune again, and the teenage girls hooted.

"Remind me to strangle the lot of them when we get back to shore," Walsh called from his duffing position. "Gifted musicians. Give me a break."

In each of the four canoes, there were positions for two paddlers and a "duffer," who lounged without a paddle in the forward midsection. Walsh duffed in one canoe with two of the boys paddling, while Amy and the third teenage boy, Homer, paddled the next. Monica and Suzi had adopted Chloe as their duffer, and Josh and Hannah paddled the fourth canoe. Their pace was slow, but up ahead the lake narrowed to a small river that would carry them beside a steep bluff half a mile to the next lake, their last.

"If the river's too high from the rain, be sure to pull up before the river," Amy called. "There's a portage on the right side. Look for the score on a pine over a sand apron. You can't miss it."

Earlier that morning she had briefed all of them on the terrain they would cover, and she wasn't worried; they'd proven themselves to be responsible and safe, drawing on the self-discipline they'd developed as musicians.

"If we smash into the granite cliff, we've gone too far, right?" Walsh called.

"Right," Amy said.

"Race you to the portage," called Monica from the bow of the girls' canoe.

Chloe began to chant a rhythm of "stroke, stroke, stroke," and the girls took off with enthusiasm, their strong young muscles propelling the canoe with a burst of speed.

"After them, you manly men," Walsh said.

Amy felt a ripple of excitement as all three canoes took off on a chase after the lead canoe, and they ate up the lake with surprising speed. She could feel the play of muscles in her arms and wrists as she timed her strokes to match those of Homer, the teenager in the front of her canoe. "Hut!" she called, and on the cue they synchronized the switch of their paddles from one side of the canoe to the other.

From both sides of the lake, the shore of trees began to narrow, and over the sound of her paddling Amy could hear another sound of water rushing. Though it was muted and distant, she was instantly afraid of what the noise signified.

"Hold up! Monica and Suzi!" she yelled. "Hold up!"

But they didn't hear her, and with their lighter load, the girls' canoe was outstripping the other three. The teenage boys with Walsh fell behind first, and Amy glanced back to see Walsh's expression of good-natured fun change to one of confusion as he began to perceive that something was wrong.

Beneath her canoe, Amy could feel the slow siphon of the lake drawing itself together to enter the river, and she could see the portage clearly marked to the right by a shelf of sand and a fallen tree. But the girls' canoe was going at the wrong angle, as if they hadn't seen it, and Amy screamed ahead to them.

"Pull over!" she yelled, plunging her paddle into the water to speed up her own canoe to catch them. "Hey! Pull over!"

From his canoe a half-length behind Amy's, Josh barked out a furious shout. "Chloe!"

Amy saw his daughter turn in her duffer's spot, her eyes round with surprise, but though she understood when Josh yelled to pull over, and she pointed to the portage, it was already too late for the older girls to steer the canoe to the side, out of danger.

"Oh, no!" Amy said. "Paddle for your life!" she yelled to Homer in the front of her canoe. "We're going after them!" She shot her gaze back toward Josh. "You pull out at the portage. The river's too high."

"We're coming too," he yelled. "Hannah, get your paddle in."

"No, Josh! It's too high! Pull over! Keep paddling, Homer!"

And then it was too late for her to look back, for the lake gave a sudden swell and their canoe was propelled over and down into the river. The water raced along the side of the bluff, more than five feet over the usual height, and fear lodged in Amy's throat. She'd paddled white water before, but never with a fully loaded canoe, and never with an inexperienced paddler in her bow. Though he must have been frightened, Homer was paddling with steady force and keeping his head up for rocks. The only way to make it down a roiling river was to paddle faster than the water was going and keep enough speed to be able to steer, for if they slowed down at all, the river would push them in its own wild direction and they would have no control.

Amy knew where the river ran toward a granite wall before making a sharp right, and as they approached it her heart raced with dread. It was all she could do to keep her canoe in control, and she knew the two teenage girls, just ahead beyond sight, wouldn't stand a chance of making it through safely.

"Stay left!" she shouted to Homer. "Stay close to the cliff!"

"No!" He began to scramble sideways with his paddle. "It's too fast! Go right!"

"Left!" She forced her paddle with all her strength through the churning water.

And then she saw them.

A hundred yards ahead, the girls' canoe had foundered to the side and was half full of water. Monica and Suzi had been swept out and were holding on for their lives. Chloe was still sitting in the duffer's spot, but since the canoe was tilted and awash with water, she was in danger of being swept downstream as soon as the canoe drifted out of the circling eddy that had captured it. Amy and Homer's canoe was shooting so close to the granite cliff, she could have reached out and touched it with her left hand. As she had predicted, the racing water closest to the cliff shot directly into the circling eddy where the girls' canoe was temporarily trapped, and Amy could feel Homer cooperating with her to pull their canoe out of the rushing river and into the circling eddy.

"Here!" she yelled, grabbing Chloe's hand and half hauling her into the canoe against her knees. In another instant she had Monica by the back of her life jacket, and Homer had locked hands with Suzi. The instant the girls let go of the swamped canoe, it made an ominous cracking noise and was slowly drifted into the current, where it tumbled with the white water around the next bend.

Amy looked into Monica's face and saw raw terror in her ragged features. The girl twisted around in her life jacket to get a better grip on Amy's canoe, and the canoe tipped dangerously to the side. Chloe screamed and lunged toward the other side. Amy strained backward, holding Monica's hand with all her might.

"You first!" Amy yelled to Homer. "Get Suzi in."

The young woman already had one knee over the gunnel, and with another heave Suzi was in the canoe, bringing a small wave of water with her. "Okay, now," Amy said to Monica. "Keep low."

The canoe was now so low in the water that it had hardly two inches of float on either side. Monica flopped in to the canoe like a fish and crammed in behind Chloe. Amy would have liked to jettison one of the packs, but she couldn't reach them with the girls in front of her, and she was afraid to do anything else to throw the canoe off balance.

She glanced at the steep shoreline, but the rock face offered no handhold, and she knew they couldn't get out there. If someone from above threw down a rope, they might have a chance, but Josh and the others weren't on this side of the river if they'd taken the portage. The only way out from the comparative safety of the circling eddy was to go down the river to the lake.

"Are you ready, Homer?" she called. "It's not much farther. Two more big bends."

"We'll never make it," Suzi said.

"Stay low, everybody," Homer said. "Ready, Amy."

Taking a deep breath, she scanned the river ahead, then made a shove with her paddle to propel the loaded canoe back out into the main current of the river. Chloe screamed again and Monica held her tight while Amy paddled with desperate strength to control the heavy, unbalanced canoe in the river. Homer was pulling the best he could, but she could feel that his strength was flagging, and as they shot past a boulder at the first bend she knew they were losing their steering capacity.

"Go, Homer! Go!" she yelled.

The second bend loomed before them, the river propelling them toward the rocks with mind-numbing speed, and Amy could see people standing on the ridge above the river. Josh and the others had run down the portage and were watching the river sweep them toward the lower lake. As the canoe turned sharply, Amy, with all her strength, jammed her paddle against the rock to keep the canoe from smashing against it. Then the river completed the final bend and opened into a wide, blue lake, spilling the canoe into calm water as suddenly as it had sucked the boat into trouble before.

Amy offered a silent prayer of thanks and steered toward the shore. As the bow of the canoe touched sand, Homer collapsed forward in the bow, his head down, his shoulders slumped with exhaustion. Suzi and Monica climbed out, dripping wet, their faces still contorted with fear, and with one look at each other, they flew into each other's arms. Chloe turned in her spot at Amy's knees and buried her face in Amy's lap, hugging her waist with all the strength in her cold little body.

"Oh, Chloe," Amy said. "I'm so sorry."

"You saved us," the girl said. "We almost died."

"No." Amy hugged her reassuringly. "You're all right."

But Chloe didn't let her go, and Amy lowered her head to kiss the girl and keep her close in her tired arms. Amy was still panting, her heart racing, and she was terribly afraid, still, of how close they'd been to disaster. When she was reaching out to the girl to rescue her from the swamped canoe, she had focused only on the urgent mechanics of the moment, but now that they were safe, now that they were hugging each other fiercely, Amy felt a connection so powerful it seemed to hammer itself against her heart, changing the shape permanently.

As she pressed her cheek against the child's wet hair and felt slender arms around her neck, she was moved by a wave of such tenderness and gratitude, she never wanted to let the girl go. "Thank God," she whispered.

The other canoe was washed up farther along the shore, in knee-deep water and possibly too damaged ever to be repaired. The gear in it was lost, swept away. But Monica and Suzi were going to be okay, and Homer . . .

"You're a star, Homer," she said.

"I'm just trying to be a manly man," he said, his voice still dry with exhaustion.

Relieved, the others laughed. Josh came close and swung Chloe up into his arms. "You okay, honey?"

"Yeah," Chloe said.

With her arms tingling from emptiness now that Chloe had released her, Amy's eyes locked with Josh's over the girl's shoulder. His cheeks were still ashen, and there was a coldness in his eyes that struck a new kind of fear through her.

"I'm sorry," Amy whispered.

There was an instant of silence before he answered. "It isn't your fault."

But it was, and she knew he blamed her no matter what he said. She'd endangered his daughter's life. She'd let Monica and Suzi endanger theirs when she let them go ahead, and there was no way for her to escape this truth. It didn't matter that the girls had charged ahead, that they'd ignored her orders to pull over to the portage. Amy should have been in the lead canoe to stop them.

Monica was looking at her hand, inspecting for damage, and Homer asked if she was okay.

"I hurt my hand." She slowly flexed her fingers.

"Let me see." Walsh took her hand.

"Which one?" Spud asked.

"My right," she said.

"Well, that's good at least," Spud said.

Amy was surprised but then realized Monica's left hand was more critical to her violin playing. Everyone checked for other injuries, but besides a few bruises and scrapes, they were all okay. Amy breathed a big sigh of relief. It was the first time anything of this magnitude had ever happened on a trip she was running, and it shook her, deeply. She was intensely grateful that nothing worse had developed.

"The pickup site is just across the lake," she said, looking across the wide expanse of sky-reflecting water. She outlined a plan for all of them to go over in the three canoes, then she could come back to tow the damaged canoe and pick up the extra packs. Everyone busied themselves rearranging the gear in the canoes, and in another hour they reached the pickup site.

The musicians had regained their high spirits by then and were already elaborating on the adventure they'd just experienced. The van wasn't there yet, so the teenagers stretched out on the rocks by the water and began finishing off the lunch supplies. The two little girls joined them with relish, and Chloe told the whole story again from her point of view as the duffer.

Amy quietly picked up her paddle and waved briefly to Walsh and Josh.

"I'm coming with you," Josh said.

"I'm fine," she said. "You can help load the canoes on the trailer when the van comes."

He looked intently at her, but the deep embarrassment she felt, the failure, made her blush and look away.

"I'm coming with," he repeated, stepping into the stern.

She frowned at him. It was one thing for him to insist on helping, another thing for him to take charge and choose the steering seat in the canoe. But when he looked up at her, an amused challenge in the curve of his lips, she grabbed her PFD and stepped into the front of the canoe.

All her life Amy had loved canoeing, and she had canoed with expert paddlers from all over the globe. She knew what it felt like to have a strong man in the stern guiding and propelling the canoe from behind her, and she knew what it was like to skim over brilliant blue water in just a spray of wind. But though she'd been in situations similar to this one thousands of times before, nothing had prepared her for the complete, perfect coming together of physical sensations that was happening with Josh in her stern.

With her knees pressed against the gunnels, her back straight and tall, she reached her paddle deep into the dark water on the right side of the canoe, so deep her fingertips met the water and the paddle moved like a natural extension of her arm. The water pushed behind her almost effortlessly because Josh had synchronized the rhythm of his paddling exactly to hers, and the combined, timed force propelled the light canoe with more grace than the most intricate ballet. She almost closed her eyes with pure pleasure, but she wanted to see it all, feel it through to her bones.

He didn't speak, even as they approached the spot where they'd left their gear and the damaged canoe, but she lifted her paddle at the very moment he, too, stopped paddling, and they skimmed silently toward the shore. Her heart was pounding, her breaths were deep and full, but she didn't dare look back at him, not yet. She didn't see how anything could be more special than this first, incredibly perfect canoeing with him, and she didn't want to end it by turning around for a summary smile.

When she finally touched her paddle against the shore and stepped out, she turned to face him, knowing her eyes were still shining with joy.

What she saw in his eyes made her lungs tighten with unexpected pain. He was watching her, yes, but instead of smiling, his expression was a mask of wary speculation. He reached up slowly to wipe a gleam of sweat from his forehead.

"What is it?" she asked.

"Nothing."

His denial made her heart plummet. Hadn't he felt what she did? As he was getting out of the canoe he deliberately avoided her gaze, and she couldn't stand not knowing what he was thinking.

"Wasn't that good?" she tried again.

"It was great," he said, still not looking at her.

"So what's the matter then?"

"Nothing," he repeated. "Let's just get the stuff and get back to Chloe and Hannah, all right?"

The sting of his practicality shattered the last of her ephemeral happiness, and she turned abruptly to load the packs into the canoe. She didn't get it. How could they be on such different wavelengths? Why was he blocking her out yet again? She felt her throat tightening as she realized his mood must be connected to Chloe and the accident, which was all her fault. How could she be so stupid?

Wordlessly, she rigged the damaged canoe to tow behind, and in another minute they were starting back across the lake. This time their canoe was loaded with three packs, and the towed canoe was sluggish behind them. Amy paddled in the bow again, but there was none of the magical pleasure from before. This was work, stubborn labor, and although she and Josh paddled in rhythm, the transcendent quality was gone.

Too many things have gone wrong, she thought, pulling hard at her paddle and feeling the wood rub against her calluses. Loving him didn't mean she understood him. Again and again she drove her paddle into the water, until finally she had to blink back a tear. It was her fault. She'd endangered his daughter and he was still in shock. How selfish could she be to think he'd care how smoothly they canoed together? Her own egotism appalled her.

When they arrived at the pick-up site, the van was there and the other canoes had already been loaded onto the trailer. Amy was surprised to see Dinah instead of Rex, and with effort she pushed her own problems to a back burner. Since Dinah occupied herself almost exclusively with Dinah's Depot and the full-time job of supplying provisions for the canoe trips, her presence at a pickup site could only mean that something was very wrong at Home Trail Outfitters. The middle-aged woman offered a wan smile that only compounded Amy's anxiety.

She waited until the last canoe and gear had been stowed, until a moment when she and Dinah were behind the van, temporarily out of ear shot from the others. "Is everything all right?" Amy asked.

Rex's daughter barely shook her head. "I'll let Dad tell you."

NINE

The hour-long ride back to the outfitters was one of the longest, bumpiest ones Amy had ever known, and the gnawing anxiety in her gut made her want to throw up. Dinah would say nothing more in front of the others. Walsh and the teenagers seemed oblivious of the mood, joking with grating cheeriness from the back of the van. Hannah and Chloe, exhausted, slept on the blue vinyl seat next to their father, who had withdrawn for reasons of his own. Much as Amy wanted to turn around in her seat and hash it out with him, what she had to say was too private.

When they pulled into the parking lot at Home Trail Outfitters, Rex barely gave her time to say good-bye to Walsh and the teenagers before he pulled her aside.

"Wait, Rex," Amy said. "I want to say good-bye to Josh and his daughters too."

Josh was holding the girls' binoculars, and his steady gaze showed he'd missed nothing of the tension between Amy and her employer.

"There's no hurry," he said. "We were going to take a look in the store."

She seriously doubted that had been his plan, and the girls looked surprised, too, but they gamely ran ahead into the store and disappeared into a tent that was set up for display. Josh idled after them, and with hardly a glance at Amy, he picked up a fishing lure with yellow feathers on it.

Amy was both glad that he was sticking around and worried that it meant he, too, knew they needed to talk. With her stomach at an all-time low, Amy followed Rex into the office and around the corner to his desk. Though the rest of the back room was large, Rex's office was crowded behind a bookshelf, with maps, model ships, birds' nests, and books piled in casual order. A manual typewriter held the place of honor in the middle of his desk, and more than once she had seen him meticulously clean black bits of ink from the letters, using a pin for the crevices in the letters. She had always admired Rex, as a craftsman who could make the sweetest canoe, as an old friend of her father's, and as a proud man of integrity and dreams.

As he sat in his old blue swivel chair and turned his face toward the window, the soft light on his chiseled features made her afraid, and she instinctively reached a hand out for his.

"What's happened?" she asked, her hushed voice revealing her concern. "You're not ill, are you?"

"No," he said, giving her hand a quick squeeze before he withdrew his own. "It's like this. I got a call this morning from Olivia at the bank. She was nice about it, but she said I had insufficient funds to cover a check that was coming through my account, and she thought it was a little irregular."

Amy sat slowly on a stool and waited for him to go on. She'd always known her friend Olivia was conscientious about her work at the bank, but she'd never have predicted what Rex next told her. The day before his account had been emptied, wiping out not only his profits for the summer but the last of his cash reserves. Everything connected to Home Trail Outfitters was cleared out, leaving him nothing but a small nest egg he'd saved for retirement.

"Is it Larry?" Amy asked.

"Who else? He didn't come into work today. He's probably half way to Fiji by now." The betrayal by his longtime friend had clearly devastated Rex, but as if the losses weren't enough of a shock, the bouncing check that Olivia held was for their insurance premium, due the day before. If it was returned unpaid to the insurance company, they would be operating illegally, without insurance, as of the previous night, at midnight.

"You mean, the accident we had on the river this morning? We weren't covered by insurance then?" Amy asked, aghast.

"No. Not if the check bounces. I sent it in on time, but if it doesn't clear, the policy expires."

Even though tragedy had been averted, there were still costs to such an accident—repair work on the canoe, X rays or other follow-up care for Monica. Insurance routinely covered these expenses, and a person had to be insane to run a business like theirs without it.

"What are we going to do?"

"I've been thinking about it all day," Rex said. "There's only one thing to do. I'm waiting until the last canoes return tomorrow, and then we're shutting down."

"You can't!"

"I don't have a choice."

But Amy refused to accept it. "If you close down, even for a couple of days, all the work we've put into this summer will be ruined. Reputation is everything, Rex."

For the first time, he seemed angry with her. "You think I haven't thought of that?"

"Then what are you saying? You'll close down permanently?"

Rex smacked his hand against the desk and stood. "We don't have a cash flow. We don't have insurance. Don't be dense, Amy. We're already out of business."

"I can't believe Larry," she said. "How could he do this?"

"We have to start calling people to tell them not to come. I have to find some way to reimburse them for their deposits."

His gentle integrity made her even more outraged. "No! There has to be a way. We've got to find Larry and get the money back. We'll call Olivia and ask the bank to hold the check or give us a loan. I'll call my mother and Nigel and get a loan from them if I have to. *Something's* got to work, but don't close down, Rex."

Rex picked up a compass, and she could see he was watching the little metal needle tremble in the case. For an instant, she had a sense of déjà vu, as if she'd seen finger and thumb on a compass before, at just that angle, in the same light, and then the impression was gone.

There was a stirring noise behind Amy and she turned sharply.

Josh's tanned cheeks were ruddy with embarrassment, but his mouth was drawn in a decisive line. "Ex-

cuse me. I happened to overhear your conversation.
Perhaps I could suggest something."

Amy was indebted to Josh on Rex's behalf, so indebted it was humbling. She tried to sort through her
feelings later that evening on the porch swing and
hardly knew where to start: There was the gratitude for
his sound advice and promises of even more assistance.
There was the aching love she'd felt for him when they
made love by the starlit lake. And there was the pene-
trating guilt for letting his daughter almost drown. She
knew he was angry with her, that he wanted to with-
draw from her, and yet he'd come forward when she
and Rex needed help most.

Word got around town that Larry had stolen money
not only from Rex, but from two other businesses that
he handled the accounting for, and it was anyone's
guess where he had disappeared to. Rumors spread that
a girlfriend was involved, despite the fact that no one
had seen Larry with a girlfriend any time in the last five
years. The jokes were running thick and fast, but if Rex
had been afraid people would shun Home Trail Outfitters, just the opposite was true. All afternoon people
had dropped by the office to offer their condolences
and help. They'd brought casseroles, as if food would
lessen the shock, and whether they'd offered cheery
support or gloomy sympathy, Rex had been visibly
moved.

What Amy felt most was exhaustion. Not even a
long shower had calmed her nerves, and she couldn't
believe she had to face Josh again so soon. When he'd
offered to come back and look at the accounts on the
computer, Rex had accepted with alacrity, and Amy had

been enlisted to assist. What Rex didn't realize was that a painful awkwardness had sprung up between her and Josh, and she didn't know how to resolve it.

When his station wagon pulled up before her house, she hurried out to forestall him from coming in and lingering. He got out of the car anyway and came around to hold the door for her.

"Hi." His mellow, low voice gave the syllable a sort of intimacy that warned her he'd been thinking about her too.

"Thanks for coming back." She slipped past his body to reach her seat, then waited while he slowly closed her door.

If she had hoped her casual gratitude would establish a neutral tone between them, she was only partly disappointed. As Josh took the wheel and began driving, he neither opened up a difficult discussion nor denied that anything was wrong. He said nothing, and the silence stretched her nerves taut.

As he drove past town, she had a flash of memory of the last time she'd been in his front seat, the day they had bought ice cream at Mindy's with his daughters. A lot had changed since that afternoon when she didn't go along on their picnic. She liked to think she knew Chloe and Hannah a lot better now. And Josh too. As they sped along the highway, the evening shadows pushing the forest trees toward the road, part of her felt as if she'd known Josh a million years, though it was only a couple of months since Briana and Lee's wedding. Another part of her felt that he was a stranger from another universe.

"Rex called," she said.

"Oh?"

She nodded. "He talked to the police, and he went

to the bank to freeze activity on his old accounts and open new ones. Like you suggested, he was able to extend his credit limit on his cash reserve, and that can act like a temporary loan until he can work out something better for the long term. Olivia's been incredibly helpful."

"Olivia seems to be a good friend to have. And a smart banker."

"He won't need to borrow your money," she said.

"That's between me and him."

She squeezed her fingers together and pressed them between the knees of her jeans.

"Its really nice of you to do this for Rex."

He glanced over briefly, then looked back out the windshield. He steered with one hand curved in the low arc of the steering wheel.

"I'm not doing this for Rex," he said.

No, of course not, she realized. She bit her lips inward as the coils in her belly tightened another notch.

"Is Chloe okay? I mean, how are they, the girls?" she asked.

"Exhausted. Filthy. Totally wired. My mother was delighted to get them."

Amy watched as the scenery raced past the window, while she felt an ache of loneliness, knowing someone else was tucking them in tonight. She hoped his mother remembered to wish the girls sweet dreams. "I'm glad," she said quietly.

He gave her another sharp look, then drove on in silence.

Amy sat up proudly, but she didn't know when she'd been more miserable. It was as if a door had closed between them somehow, and it seemed totally backward to her. She cared about him more than ever, and she was certain she was important to him. Why couldn't they talk about what really mattered between them?

Several miles later, they pulled into the parking lot of Home Trail Outfitters, and though it was nearly eight-thirty, the sky was still lit by the setting sun. The office door was locked, but there were lights on inside, and Dinah let them in.

"Hi," she said. "I wasn't sure if you were still going to make it."

"I had to get my daughters home to Blue Gill," Josh said. "I just got back."

Dinah nodded, her eyes flicking to Amy. Dinah seemed to realize something, and Amy felt a sudden awkwardness among the three of them.

"How's Rex?" Amy asked.

"He's asleep, actually," Dinah said. "It was a big day, and when I saw him nodding off, I told him to go upstairs and watch TV. It would be good if he could sleep awhile."

Amy agreed.

"Any word on Larry?" Josh asked.

Dinah preceded them into the back room, shaking her head. "No. The police have sent a description of him to the Minneapolis–St. Paul airport, but I don't think it will help much. It's not like he's a big killer and they can afford a huge manhunt."

"He's just Larry," Amy said.

"Exactly." Dinah smiled for the first time that night. "Listen, I made a big pot of chili. Want some?"

Amy looked at Josh, and the tension in his jaw eased as he smiled and accepted the invitation. The three of them ate chili and some of the banana bread a friend had brought, and while the tension between Amy and

Josh didn't vanish entirely, it was eased somewhat by the delicious food and Dinah's comforting presence. At least they were able to look each other in the eye without scrutinizing each other.

After Dinah went up to keep her father company, Amy and Josh started on the computer. Amy had already spent hours that afternoon looking at the files and checking the manuals, and it was with both envy and relief that she saw Josh click quickly through the menus on the screen. She secretly vowed to expand her knowledge of computer accounting programs. Pulling a chair close, she was careful to keep her knee from touching his, and they gazed at the computer monitor together, their faces faintly illuminated by the same gray glow.

Behind them, the back office was orderly and quiet, except for an occasional hum from the fluorescent lights overhead. On the screen door a moth clung unnoticed, while the forest offered up its chant of crickets and birds. Windows facing the lake let in a soft breeze and the occasional buzz of a dragonfly feasting on mosquitoes. Darkness slowly turned the green of the willow tree by the brook to a soft gray and the pines to a deeper gray, while mist slowly covered the lake. Amy noticed the changes only when she got up to close the windows and keep back the chill, and she pulled on an old burgundy cardigan that had been left on a hook by the door.

Josh looked up from the computer. "Warm enough?"

"I'm fine," she said, but shivered. "Bad news always makes me cold."

"Yeah. I think it's getting worse, too."

Led by Josh's pointed questions, she quoted figures

from the written records and receipts in the files. By cross-checking with Larry's computer entries, they discovered a dozen times in the last three years when Larry had transferred money to a cash account where it had vanished. Though each amount itself wasn't large, over the years it added up to a considerable sum—a sum that would have meant a respectable profit to Rex. Instead his business had slowly been destroyed.

"Rex isn't going to be happy about this," Josh said. "Larry has been stealing from him for years."

"I just don't get it," Amy said. "If Larry's been skimming money off Rex and two other businesses, he must be loaded. Why, all the sudden, would he decide to take off?"

He turned in his chair to face her and linked an arm over the chair back. "Was somebody about to find him out?"

Amy inspected a red button on the sweater and tried to think. "Rex, maybe. He started to learn how to use the computer this summer."

"And what about this girlfriend rumor?"

She looked up, puzzled. "I don't know anything about it. He's always been very private about his personal life."

"Uh-oh," he said. "I have an idea."

He pivoted back to the computer and began moving the mouse. A little light on the modem went on, followed by an amplified dial tone that sounded oddly high-tech in the outfitters' office.

"Do you have E-mail here?" he asked, frowning.

"No," she said. "At least, I never thought we did."

He searched through several settings in the menu, then slumped back. "I bet anything Larry has an E-mail account," he said. "Does he have a computer at home?"

"Yes," she said. "He does a lot of our accounting out of his home, actually."

He sat up again, pulled up an Internet search engine, and began typing. In half a dozen attempts, he located Larry's E-mail address. "Yes!"

As she watched his profile, she realized she was glimpsing what Josh must be like when he was working. He'd been playing on computers for years. And he designed computer games, for goodness' sake. Before, the idea had intimidated her, or rather, it made her feel how different he was from her. Now his computer expertise was just another aspect of his multi-faceted personality, in balance with his other qualities just as her canoeing expertise was only part of who she was.

"What are you doing now?" she asked.

"Cracking into his E-mail."

"Isn't that illegal?"

"Unethical, certainly. But since the man just wiped out Rex's business, I'd say we're entitled to any info we can get."

When she thought of Rex upstairs, asleep from stress and exhaustion, she found she couldn't argue with Josh's morals. In another moment Josh sat back again, victorious.

"We've got him!" he said. "Look at this, Amy! It's better than I imagined!"

She had to lean forward to read the tiny script on the computer:

Yo, Larry, get a life. I'm sorry if you've been deluding yourself, but there's no way I'm meating you in Grand Kayman or anywhere else. Don't take this wrong, you seemed like a nice enough guy, but a on-line relationship was all I was looking for and you

*should of understood. Incredible. My sister's going to
freak when I tell her. Signing off for good,*

Pam:(

Despite herself, Amy laughed. "Oh my gosh. He
had a computer girlfriend and she can't even spell."

"She used a sideways sad face," he said. "Looks bad
for Larry. He must have left last night just before this
message posted, and I'd bet anything he never even
read it. At least now we can tell the police where he's
going."

Amy exhaled on a long breath. "Rex will be so relieved. Do you think there's any chance of getting the
money back?"

"I don't know," he said.

It would mean so much to Rex. She had already
convinced him they could salvage the business despite
their losses, but it would be an uphill climb. She listened for noise from upstairs, but the room was still,
and not even the hum of the TV could be heard anymore.

"Rex reminds you of your father, doesn't he?" he
asked.

"I guess he does."

"And in a way, you saved him today when you convinced him not to close his business. It's not really the
same thing, but that's part of it, isn't it?"

She reached for the compass Rex had left on the
desk and didn't answer right away. "I hadn't thought of
that. Saving Rex's business isn't the same thing as saving my father, of course. My father's gone. There was
no way to save him." It made her uneasy to talk to Josh
about her father this way, and she tried to redirect the
topic.

She gestured at the E-mail message still on the monitor. "No wonder Larry never talked about his girl-friend," she said. "If the guys had known, they would have teased him ruthlessly."

He stretched in his chair, and then he gazed at her with a curious smile. "Do you have anyone teasing you about me?"

Besides herself? Josh Kita was way beyond teasing material. She stood and paced around the map table to provide an outlet for her pent-up energy.

"Amy? Have you talked to people about me?"

She gave the compass a little toss and tried to hedge. "I don't exactly need to talk about you."

He crossed his arms over his chest and his eyebrows arched upward. "Who all knows?"

She tilted her face slightly as she thought about her answer. "There's my mother. And my bridge friends, of course. And my brother, Sean. A couple of my guy friends here at the outfitters have accused me of being, well, clueless lately. Then there's Walsh."

"Oh, yes. Our troubadour."

She lifted the metal compass and pressed it absently against her cheek. "How did you like Walsh?"

"You mean, was I jealous?"

She gave a brief laugh, then looked up at him with frank curiosity. "Well, were you?"

"Only insecure, distrustful men are jealous."

"Oh," she said. She frowned down at her hiking boots, noting with annoyance that the leather was due for more bear grease to keep it supple.

Josh rose silently from his chair. "On the other hand," he said, "if it was Walsh who'd met you by the lake last night instead of me, it might be a different story."

Low in her chest, her heart began to thud oddly. "You're saying you might be jealous if I kissed someone else?"

He stepped a few paces toward her. "We did more than kiss."

"You like this slow approach, don't you?" She watched the lazy grace of his body as he approached. "You tried it on me in my own kitchen once." And she knew what had happened after that.

He walked around the edge of the table. "Do you find it unnerving?"

She swallowed hard. "It does make me feel a little like you're a cat and I'm a nice juicy mouse."

"Then back away."

She knotted her fingers in the hem of the sweater, feeling her adrenaline course down her spine, setting all her nerve endings on hyperalert. His feet made no noise over the hardwood floor, and his hands were dropped in his pockets with deceptive, casual ease.

"I can't," she said softly.

"What?"

She felt her throat grow dry, and licked her lips. There was no way she could tell him she was already captured by his advance, and that backing up was no more physically possible than leaping to the moon. "Don't you think, for once, we should try to talk through our differences before you knock my sense clear out of my head with a kiss?"

He stopped advancing and his lips curved in a wary half smile. "What if I say no?"

In desperation, she said the most honest thing she could think of. "I couldn't bear it when you were mad at me. After the accident."

He started as if she had struck him, and then he

regarded her with such fierce intensity he frightened her.

"You can't imagine how furious I was." His voice was low.

Her heart leaped in new terror, and she knew then that she hadn't imagined his fury when she almost let his daughter drown. "I know," she whispered, her throat constricting with emotion. "I know."

"Damn." He grabbed her arms and crushed his mouth against hers in a torrid, demanding kiss. She was stunned by his punishing need, but she responded with equal passion, as if she could prove how much she cared by refusing to back down. She arched against him, matching him inch for inch, even as his grip bit into her arms.

When he wrenched himself away from her, she stumbled and had to brace herself on the table behind her. Her loose blond hair slid forward around her face, and she touched her fingers to her tender lips.

"I don't understand," she said.

He shook his head, unable to articulate a response. Then he gazed across the room toward the dark windows, his face inscrutable. When another long moment ticked by and he still didn't answer, a rebellious fire of resentment kindled and flamed in her soul. She tried to keep her voice gentle, but her emotion gave it an edge of urgency.

"I'm sorry, Josh."

"I know. It was as much my fault as anyone's when I let her get in the other canoe with Suzi and Monica. That's not it."

She still didn't understand. "Then what is it?"

She could see he was torn, and then he deliberately decided not to explain something to her, something about his daughters. Hurt cleaved neatly through her heart, and she swallowed hard over the pain. All right, it was true. She wasn't responsible enough to be trusted with his daughters. Or with him.

He might make love to her and tell her he loved her, but when it came right down to it, he didn't trust her with the intimate secrets of his heart. He didn't need to say it out loud.

She had never dreamed that a silent rejection could be so powerful. She had to find a way out of this labyrinth, for both of them. "It's normal to have doubts."

"You have them," he said, then waited, as if his statement were really a question, begging to be refuted.

A ripping sensation went through her, but finally she nodded.

Josh turned slowly to pace toward the windows, and she could hear the faintly audible rustle of keys in his trousers, which signaled he'd slid a hand in his pocket as he always did. When he spoke, his voice was keenly sardonic. "You want to give me a hint of what I'm up against here? The wanderlust?"

Her cheeks burned, and she had a fleeting memory of telling him she dreamed of spending every night in a different campsite. "That isn't fair."

"Then tell me what is." He turned to face her. He was like a tiger, ready to devour her or swat her away like a pesky fly. "This isn't enough anymore. If it were just myself, I could play the game a little longer. But I can't risk my daughters with you anymore, not after the canoe trip."

She couldn't believe he could be so brutal. "I *said* I was sorry."

His face paled and his lips closed in a grim line. "I

meant, I can't risk having them love you, when I can't guarantee you'll stay in their lives for good."

Cold, searing shame knifed through her as she realized the enormity of her mistake. "We never should have started this. I should have just let you kiss me so we'd never—" She stopped and bit back her words. "I'm sorry. I put that badly."

He laughed briefly. "Clear as a scalpel, actually."

Her cheeks burned and her mind raced with confusion and embarrassment, but she couldn't leave him thinking she didn't care. She could feel a silent countdown beginning, and knew without a doubt that he was about to turn around and walk out the door. She forced herself toward him and placed her fingers on his arm. It had worked before, ages ago at Lake Eloise, when she'd hardly known him. Please, she thought.

She saw his gaze on her slender fingers, and a faint blush tinged his cheeks.

"Don't bother trying to seduce me," he said. "I don't believe in casual sex."

It took forever for her mind to fully comprehend what he was saying, for the hurt to penetrate, but then it hit with lashing force. She flinched, then turned blindly. Unable to breathe, she walked slowly to the back door but her shaky legs forced her to stop beside the blackened windows.

She struggled for a last shred of dignity. "Please leave, then."

In the silence, his footsteps were loud as he left the room and closed the door.

TEN

With a savage heart and cold control, Josh flipped pancakes at his stove. The school bus was due in ten minutes, and besides breakfast, they still needed hair combed, snacks, and shoes. He slid the last hot pancakes onto their plates, poured syrup, and cut Hannah's into neat squares. When he started to cut Chloe's, she waved him off.

"I can do it myself," she said.

Unsmiling, he glanced at her serious face and forced himself to soften his expression. "Good."

Chloe pushed her glasses up her nose and eyed him skeptically.

"You should go for a run or something," his daughter said. "Work it out."

He rubbed a hand along the stubble on his jaw. "Work what out?"

She pointed her fork at him and talked with her mouth full. "*You* know."

"What?" Hannah asked. "Did he talk to Amy yet? I can spell Amy. Listen."

As she intoned the three letters, giving them all capital status with her childish voice, Josh groaned and reached for the hair brush. "You guys have two minutes to get out to the bus," he said.

"When are we going to see her?" Hannah asked, enduring the ministrations of the hairbrush as she forked up her last bite of her breakfast. "I never got to show her how I can swim yet."

"Yeah, Dad," Chloe said. "When are we going to see Amy?"

"I don't know. All right?"

"Well, don't get mad at *us*," Chloe said.

"I'm not mad."

But it made him angry just to think about Amy. Knowing it wasn't fair to be cranky with the girls, he focused on the final rush of hurrying them into shoes and backpacks. He checked their faces, then gave them each a kiss before they ran through the living room to the front door. The sculpture clock over the mantel bonged eight-fifteen. As Hannah and Chloe ran down the long driveway, he followed more slowly, joining them just as the bus breaked to a squeaky halt before their home.

Hannah turned halfway up the steps of the bus to look back and smile at him. "I have an idea, Daddy," she said. "You can use your *words* with Amy. That's what we do when we're mad at school."

"Very nice suggestion, pumpkin. Thanks."

To hell with words. Waving them good-bye, he pulled the newspaper out of the delivery box and started slowly back up the drive.

He didn't miss her. She'd been nothing but trouble since the minute she came crying down the aisle at Lee and Briana's wedding. He should have known then she was the last sort of woman he should get mixed up with.

It's normal to have doubts, she'd said.

Like hell it was.

An image of her paddling in the bow of his canoe passed before him and blocked out his view of the familiar driveway: her tanned shoulders and the deep expanse of her back between the straps of her blue one-piece swimsuit, the muscles of her arms handling the paddle like a bird used wings, her blond braid swinging gently with the rhythm that rocked all the way through him from his groin to his heart. Her innate beauty first delighted him, as if the memory were a gift, but then her image receded ahead of him, smaller and smaller into the distance. She was so true and strong and wild, like the water or the sky. Always just ahead, beyond reach, facing away from him.

He ground his feet into the gravel as he approached his house, then balked at the idea of going inside where his work was waiting for him. His home, his routine, his whole life seemed like a trap. He could imagine years and years unfolding before him, his girls going off every morning on the bus, going through grade school, then middle school, then beyond. And he'd still be stuck, alone, while Amy Larkspur adventured through her own life without him.

"Damn."

He pivoted and strode to the big pine where the girls' swings hung, each with a crescent of dew trapped in the curve. He idly wrapped his fingers around one of the ropes, welcoming the coarse thickness.

There were only about five million things he should have said to her the other night. Like, "Hannah's adored you since the first time you gave her a Popsicle," and "Since you saved Chloe's life, you're the closest thing to a mother she's ever likely to get."

He had been furious when Chloe almost drowned, but it didn't make him trust Amy any less, and that was what shocked him. He tried to think how he would have felt if anyone else had been in charge of the trip, or if, for that matter, Shannon had ever endangered his daughters. His fury and his need to assign blame would have made the distance between himself and that person insurmountable. Yet with Amy, after his initial horror had passed, he had known it truly was an accident, nobody's fault but the river's.

That was what disturbed him the most. When had he come to trust her so completely? When had he started to want to share responsibility for the girls with her? Not just as a babysitter or friend, but as an equal parent, a mother who would care for them and cherish them and guide them with her own character, her own strengths and flaws. Amy was too dynamic to hover as a hesitant stepmother, politely doing laundry in the background. She would sweep them into her life, haul them out on the trail, feed them fudge, teach them bridge, and give them the heritage of her own voyageur heart.

We never should have started this, she'd said.

Her words circled mercilessly in his thoughts.

There was no "we" about it. He had pursued her relentlessly, despite her bridge group, despite her friendly guys, despite her sex-for-fun whimsy that had almost killed him. He had shoved himself into her life, her canoe, the lifeblood of her business, her memories of her father, even into her bed. And she still could stand before him and suggest he must have normal doubts.

Talk about a nasty crash factor.

He tried to think why the feeling was familiar, but when he thought of Shannon, awareness replaced his bitterness. They're not the same, he reminded himself. Shannon really hadn't cared for him, and when their marriage had failed, he'd scorned both himself and his ex-wife for the failure. But Amy was sincere; she did have doubts and she really did care for him. He knew that. His own, old pattern of withdrawal was what was hurting him most now, and as he thought back on the other times he'd withdrawn from Amy, when he'd said, "Nothing's wrong," when something actually was, he realized that on some unconscious level, he hadn't trusted Amy not to be like Shannon.

A big mistake. There was nothing about Amy that deserved his bitterness.

He shouldn't have said that he didn't believe in casual sex, even though it was true. A nobler man would have answered her sweet, unspoken offer of friendly understanding with a new infusion of patience.

He frowned at the dirt between his shoes and released the swing. He'd never be that virtuous.

He could have warned her not to touch him again unless she promised to marry him. That was what he really wanted.

An image of her laughing floated before him, taunting him. *So now you're reduced to blackmail,* he could hear her say.

It wasn't blackmail. It was a proposal.

Then again, at this point, he'd use whatever worked.

Amy leaned into the handle of her lawn mower and started it down the slope of her side yard. Clippings flew out of the vent, the noise was terrific, and the gas fumes far overpowered the smell of cut grass, at least at the start. When she got to the edge of the grass, she turned, and with one hand hauled the machine behind her, making no effort to mow as she went up. Back at the top, she repositioned the mower and started down again on a swatch next to the first.

She liked the way the noise blasted all thought out of her head, so she didn't have to think about anything difficult. Make that any*body* difficult. She could concentrate on the green lines of the lawn and the ache in her calf muscles, rather than on whether the phone was going to ring. As she pushed at the hair in her face, she accidentally wiped a blade of grass against her nose. Then the mower, always problematic, conked out.

"Shoot."

She checked the choke button, took a grip on the black handle, and gave a full pull to the rip cord. The motor chugged pathetically and refused to start. She took a deep breath, pulled again, and still it didn't start. Unreasoning anger boiled through her veins, and she grabbed the handle with both hands, wrenching it outward with all her strength.

"Damn it all to hell!" She released the cord, and it snapped back into the dead motor.

What was she doing? What on earth was wrong with her? The stupid thing was just out of gas again—no big deal. She sat down abruptly in the long grass and covered her face with her fingers.

"I ought to wring his neck," she whispered viciously.

She wasn't any good at this idiotic silence game.

She knew he'd called Home Trail Outfitters, but he hadn't asked for her. Instead, Rex had given Josh the update on how the police were hoping to apprehend

Larry in Grand Cayman. Rex had named Dinah a co-owner of his business, and cautious optimism covered their outlook for the rest of the summer. While Amy hovered anxiously, waiting for Rex to pass over the phone, he had signed off and looked up at her, apologetic.

"He didn't want to speak to you," Rex said.

Since then, another forty-eight hours had unfolded with no call, no friendly dropping by, no nothing. What did she expect? He'd done this before and obviously thought nothing of going for days without talking to her. Why should the situation be any different now? The man was a master at cryptic messages and games; he thrived on them. She should know better than to try to figure him out, especially after his last parting insult about casual sex.

She wanted to smash something. A big window, for instance. Her fingers closed on a stick, and she hurled it thirty yards toward the shed where it struck within an inch of the window, then fell harmlessly to the ground.

Even her aim was off. That was his fault too.

She stood up and marched down to the shed, intending to get the spare gallon of gasoline and muscle her way through the rest of the lawn. But when she opened the door to the shed, her hope canoe was waiting in the quiet dimness of the interior, and her sneakers slowed to a stop. The canoe seemed to have grown in the weeks since she'd seen it with Josh, until the arching, golden shape was almost alive, pleading with her like a locked-up puppy. "Let me out!" it seemed to say. "Don't leave me here alone in the shed!"

Every old dream she'd ever had came tumbling around her like the dust motes that streamed in the small square window.

Gas can forgotten, Amy bit her lips together and stepped cautiously forward, and when she slowly set her fingers on the satiny wood of the canoe her father had so lovingly made for her, all the false anger and defenses she'd built inside her began to crumble. Long-denied tears trembled near the surface of her consciousness, and she had to sniff hard to hold them back.

"Oh, Daddy."

If only he were still there to advise her.

She'd heard that children who lost a parent grieved for them over and over, at different developmental stages, so a preschooler who lost a mother would deal with loss again as a young child, as a pubescent, and as an adolescent. In a way, Amy felt she'd reached another milestone this summer, and her father was mixed up in it too.

She tried to think rationally, then remembered the afternoon with Cottie at the post office, when she'd first pondered the links between Chloe and Josh and her own father. Now it was obvious to her that Chloe's trouble mirrored her loss, and that when she saw Josh patiently helping his daughter heal, an echo of that healing resonated in her own old wound.

And it went deeper than that. As Josh had pointed out, the resemblance between her father and Rex was more subtle than she'd wanted to admit. Her emotional involvement with Home Trail Outfitters had been almost unhealthy in its intensity. She'd put her whole heart into the business, neglected her friends for it, and even tied her own hope canoe dreams to it. In some way perhaps she had been trying to undo the failure of her father's death. Maybe, as an adult, she'd still hoped to erase the loss she'd felt, seeing her bewildered father in a laundry room, looking for a compass.

It didn't have to make tidy sense, she realized. Saving Rex's business could never bring her father back to life, but on some emotional level, she did feel a sense of resolution. Rex and Dinah, father and daughter, would continue a business that would keep her own heritage alive for future generations, just as her father would have wanted.

Amy slid her palm down the side of the canoe, then slowly turned and stepped toward the door and the rectangle of sunlight that fell on the worn planks.

So if she could understand it all intellectually, why did she feel so lonely?

Don't be a fool, Aim. A barrage of memories flooded through her mind to torment her: dancing with him under the mirror ball at Briana and Lee's wedding, his reverse Romeo position in the window at his home when she was on the ladder, his lips white with ice cream at Mindy's, canoeing with him in perfect synchronization, and the night by the lake when he'd made love to her under the stars like some magnificent god of the forest.

Despite his mind games, he'd been as consistent as the North Star he said he was looking for, patiently and persistently drawing her into his life, even when she resisted by backing out of his picnic, even when she almost let his daughter drown.

She groaned aloud and gripped her hand in the hair over her forehead. What was she going to do about Hannah and Chloe? While Hannah was an adorable, perfect gem of sunshine, Chloe would always be mercurial, and the two together were irresistible. Under the influence of their squabbles and sweet humor, Amy's facade of detached friendliness hadn't lasted long. It had been so hard seeing Chloe unhappy about her skating teacher, about life in general, when Amy wanted so desperately to reach in with her own love and understanding. If only she could save the little girl from her emotional extremes the way she'd saved Chloe from the swamped canoe. Amy knew it wasn't that simple, but she wanted the right to be a long-term influence in Chloe's life, just as she wanted to cherish Hannah as the girl grew and matured.

Amy stepped out of the doorway of the shed, back into the sunlight of her backyard. Okay, so what doubts, really, did she have? Fear of beginning something new, maybe. Fear of becoming a wife and a mother simultaneously. Her belly did a half roll, and she knew she was getting warm.

Then again, a new life was just one step after another, one trail leading to another, and that was what she'd always loved most. Change itself wasn't a bad thing; it was just change. And while her former life had been nice enough, the next one could include Hannah and Chloe. And Josh.

Oh my God, she thought.

Josh wasn't asking her to turn into someone perfect. He understood her, her faults and her old grief, her healing and her independence. He didn't want her to give up who she was. He wanted her to be who she was, the best she could be, with him.

This was what he meant by seeing her as the North Star. Not as a physically fixed, tied-down person, but as a constant force, part of a love so strong it would survive and grow through unforseeable changes in direction.

"Oh my God," she said. Panic charged around her head. "I'm thinking about marriage and he hasn't even proposed."

We need to have this conversation together, she thought.

She strode rapidly up the side yard toward the house. She was going to pick up her keys, grab her purse, and start driving. A glance at her watch told her she'd be at Josh's place in Blue Gill by dinnertime if she got moving. Her stomach lurched with dread and excitement. She wouldn't even call. She'd just show up as if she belonged there. She'd just—

She stopped in her tracks.

"Your mower's out of gas," Josh said, looking up with the gas cap still between two fingers.

Her smile began at her toenails and carried right through to the ends of her hair. He had never, ever looked as irresistible as he did just then with the late afternoon sunlight streaming around him and the old lawn mower next to his knee. His blue-patterned shirt fit square across his broad shoulders, and while his smile flashed with humor, the bemused irony in his gaze concealed a hint of unrequited longing. She knew that expression of his. She'd been seeing it for weeks without recognizing fully what it meant.

But she knew now. His love for her was written in every masculine inch of his body, and just being near him brought out an answering femininity in hers. Walking slowly, letting her hips move with the liquid grace she'd felt once in a bridesmaid dress, she was going to make him rue the last words he'd said about seduction.

"How nice of you to drop by," she said.

He raised one slow eyebrow, instantly alert. "I was in the neighborhood."

Liar, she thought.

"How are things with Rex?" he asked.

"He's fine. Business is steady. Now that nobody's

stealing any more, the profits should add up just fine. We're even having a sort of reunion celebration at the end of the summer for previous guests."

"That's nice," he said, although Josh didn't look as if he was listening at all.

She gestured at the gas cap. "Thanks for the diagnosis."

"Do you always mow your lawn?"

"Only when the grass gets long."

"I meant, doesn't your brother or somebody else do it for you?"

She put one hand on her hip and looked quizzically at him. "Some man, you mean?"

From the way he looked at her, she was excruciatingly aware of her slender body, from the blades of grass on her tennis shoes and her scuffed knee to the neckline of her tank top and untidy hair, and everywhere in between. He took a step toward her over the soft, unmowed grass, and she instantly recognized the game.

"Mowers and men usually go together," he said.

She smiled slowly. "What makes you think there's anything usual about me or my mower?"

"Ah," he said. "Now that's the question of the day."

He strolled one step closer, and she reached up to brush a strand of blond hair away from her eyes.

"It's been ninety-nine hours since I saw you," he said lightly. "I counted."

Her heart gave a twist. "Oh, Josh."

"The girls want to know when you're coming to see them."

For the first time, Amy's gaze faltered, and she linked her fingers together behind her back.

"How are they?" she asked.

"Okay. Lonely. Like someone else I know."

She looked back up at him and saw his smile was strained at the corners. Me, too, she thought, but the words couldn't come out.

"Have you thought at all about what we discussed the other night, or have you been too busy mowing?" he asked.

Her heart ached as she laughed. "I've thought about it a little."

She noticed he wasn't advancing toward her anymore, as if he'd forgotten his game of cornering her, or as if he'd reached some invisible barrier that kept him six feet away. He ran his fingers through the hair over one ear, then dropped his hand in his pocket.

"I know it's soon, but we've been through a lot, Amy, and I don't just mean the canoe accident. Ever since that night at the wedding, you've helped me with my daughters in ways you don't even know. I thought I was fine the way I was, but you've shown me how to be a better person. More giving, I guess."

She shook her head in denial. "I haven't done anything."

His gray eyes glowed with hidden fire. "I'm trying to say something here."

She held back a laugh. "Sorry."

When he posed one hand on his hip and frowned at her, she lifted her eyebrows with studied innocence.

"There's the way you've changed me, and then what you've done for the girls." He spoke as if consulting a memorized list, which, of course, he was. "And what we're like in bed together, and the honest, quiet side of you that matches mine, and the way we argue—that's always fun—and—"

"The answer's yes!" she interrupted. A rush of love

flowed through her and she smiled as if she would burst.

"What?"

"Yes," she repeated. "Aren't we having the same conversation? Isn't this what you've been asking me all along?"

"I was going to propose."

"I know! And the answer's yes!" She plunged forward, throwing herself in his arms, and he swung her around in a terrific embrace. He let out a shout of triumph, then crushed her mouth against his, kissing her so hard she gave up trying to breathe at all.

"You're incredible," he said. "I can't believe it."

"I can't wait to be married to you."

"Hannah and Chloe are going to be thrilled."

"So will my mother."

"You really mean it?" he asked. "Do you know what this means?"

She sobered slightly and leaned back in his arms to gaze into his eyes. With one finger, she traced the line of his mouth, loving the way it played a smile, just for her.

"I love you, Josh," she said. "I always will. I want to spend every day with you, no matter what happens, no matter where we go."

"Let's stay home together for a while," he said.

She smiled. "That sounds good to me."

He kissed her again, and she swooned against him, finally abandoning herself permanently to the vertigo. His arms were tight around her, so warm and strong, and so full of the music in her heart she felt as if they were dancing.

"I have something for you." He reached into his pocket.

When Amy saw the small paper box, she recognized it as folded origami like the paper canoe he'd given her. "What is it?" When she lifted it between her thumb and forefinger, she was surprised to hear it rattle once. "A buoy for the hope canoe?"

"In a way," he said. "Open it and see."

"Game master."

"Just open it."

Pulling apart the white creases, Amy peeked inside to where a glitter winked back. Oh my God, she thought, as the blood ran out of her face. "It's a ring," she whispered.

"For you."

She took it out of the paper and laid in on her palm, staring at it as the golden sunlight circled in the band and sent a scatter of reflections through the diamond. Josh laughed softly and retrieved it from her trembling hand.

"It's supposed to go on your finger." He slid the band over her slender knuckle.

Amy gazed down at the ring on her finger and marveled at how pretty it was, but it couldn't compare to the depth of feeling she had for the man who had given it to her. "When did you get this?"

He laughed again and pulled her close in his arms again. "You mean, how long have I known? Since the night we first made love."

"When you told me about the Kita star?"

He nodded, and his eyes were so close, she could look into the perfect black circles of his irises. "I bought it the next morning."

Amy was so moved, she couldn't speak. She gazed up at the sky, half expecting it to be evening already so she could find the North Star shining overhead, but the golden afternoon light pooled around them, July-warm and steady. And then she realized, even though she couldn't see it, the North Star was up there beyond the pale blue dome. Josh had loved her all that time, and deep inside she'd known it even while hiding it from herself.

She fingered a strand of blond hair out of her eyes and smiled up at him, loving every millimeter of his handsome face.

"I can't wait to get you in a canoe again," she said, thinking of how perfectly they'd paddled together.

"The hope canoe?" he asked.

"Absolutely."

His eyebrows lifted. "Alone?"

Then again, she thought, maybe they didn't need to paddle. As a rush of seductive pleasure rose through her, she gave him her most rakish smile. She'd hope-lessly lost her voyageur heart.

"Very alone," she agreed.

EPILOGUE

The Following Summer

Amy pushed the hope canoe out into the broad, slow river, and settled quickly in the stern to relish the first dip of her paddle into the water. It was an achingly beautiful morning, and the bright sunlight on the water exactly mirrored the happiness in her heart. The canoe slipped sweetly over the clear water, carrying her family with all the grace that her father ever could have wished for. Chloe paddled in the bow, while Josh and Hannah made the most of the duffer's life.

"Did you bring any fudge?" Hannah asked.

"It's with the picnic," Amy said.

Josh shifted to reach into the basket. "In here?"

"Hey, Chloe," Hannah said a moment later. "Dad's found the fudge."

When Chloe stopped paddling and turned to watch over her shoulder, drops of water fell from her paddle blade and shone in the sunlight.

Amy felt an odd flash of emotion, and paused to rest

her own paddle on her knees. She still could hardly believe her good fortune in having such a wonderful husband and such incredible daughters. No gift could ever match the simple, heady happiness of being with her family like this. Was it really only a year since she'd met Josh Kita?

They'd married at Thanksgiving, surrounded by family and bridge friends and a swarthy group from the outfitters. Chloe had been Amy's maid of honor, and Hannah the flower girl, and Briana had come with Lee and cried harder than anyone else.

Amy and Josh had agreed to spend the winter in Blue Gill where the girls were in school. From there, she'd found work as a naturalist for schools and winter camps, and Josh flew her whenever she needed to commute far. She loved the time with him in his plane, watching the frozen landscape pass far below. The view matched the way her life had expanded and changed through loving him.

As soon as summer arrived, they'd moved back to Amy's place so she could be closer to her work and Sean's family. Josh set up a small office in the dining room where once he'd learned to play bridge. Figuring out the logistics of where to live had been simple compared to the adjustments of learning to be a family, and Amy had been discouraged at times, but she and Josh had faced the challenges together, becoming even closer in the process.

There had been one casualty. Rover the bird hadn't made it.

Josh turned sideways to hand her a sliver of chocolate fudge and his leg nudged against her feet. "Where are you off to?" he asked.

She let sweet chocolate melt down her throat. "You

know, it's Lee and Briana's anniversary. We met a year ago today."

He lifted one eyebrow. "Did you think I'd forget?" He reached in his daypack and pulled out a tissue parcel.

"What is it? Let me see," Chloe said.

"It's a pair of moccasins!" Hannah said as Amy opened them.

"Don't worry," Josh said. "I have some for you and Chloe back at the house." He smiled at Amy and set a kiss on her bare knee. "Don't look so shocked. Just because you have no surprise for me is no reason to feel bad."

"But I do have a surprise," she said.

"What? A new handkerchief?"

"Something bigger." She tried not to let her voice give it away.

Josh tilted his head curiously and circled her kneecap with his fingers. "Would this be something bigger than a bread box?"

"Not at first," she said.

Josh's fingers gripped her knee with sudden strength and his gaze shot to hers. "You're not—"

But she couldn't keep it a secret any longer. She felt her whole face would burst with grinning so hard. "Yes," she said. "I am."

Josh pulled her into an embrace so hard that the canoe rocked precariously and the girls screamed.

"What is it? What is it?" Chloe demanded.

For the moment, Hannah was the only one able to reply. "I think we're getting a new bird."

THE EDITORS' CORNER

To celebrate our fifteenth anniversary, we have decided to couple this month with a very special theme. For many, the paranormal has always been intriguing, whether it's mystical convergences, the space-time continuum, the existence of aliens, or speculation about the afterlife. We went to our own LOVESWEPT authors and asked them to come up with their most intriguing ideas. And thus the EX-TRAORDINARY LOVERS theme month was born. Have fun with this taste of the supernatural, but first check beneath the bed, then snuggle under the covers. And don't let the bedbugs bite . . . they do exist, you know!

Brianne St. John is finding herself **NEVER ALONE,** in Cheryln Biggs's LOVESWEPT #890. It's hard enough when just one ghost is hanging around, but what does a girl do when four insistent ghosts are on her case? Ever since she was a little girl, she's had Athos, Porthos, Aramis, and yes, even D'Artagnan to scare all her boyfriends away. Now that gorgeous entrepreneur Mace Calder has set foot in Leimonte Castle, the four musketeers are in an uproar! Mace has noticed that the lady of the house tends to mutter to herself a great deal, but for now he has other important matters to take care of. As Mace and Brianne draw closer, strange things keep happening, objects are being moved, shadows are darkening doorways—and Mace wonders just when is that wall going to answer Brianne? Cheryln Biggs revisits old haunts and legends in this enchanting romp of a love story!

Journalist Nate Wagner has his hands full when he confronts **WITCHY WOMAN** Tess DeWitt, in LOVESWEPT #891 by Karen Leabo. What strikes Nate about the beautiful woman he's followed into a Back Bay antique shop is that she doesn't look like the notorious Moonbeam Majick, a witch who disappeared fifteen years ago. Tess knew she and everyone around her were in harm's way the minute she came across the cursed cat statue that had very nearly ruined her life. Teamed up with an insatiably curious Nate, Tess must find a way to save her best friend's life, prevent Nate from dying, and keep the cat away from the mysterious stranger who's bent on unleashing the statue's unholy powers. In the end, will a spell cast from loving hearts be enough to save them all from certain death? Karen Leabo delves into the mystical connections our souls offer to those we truly love.

Loveswept veteran Peggy Webb gives us **NIGHT OF THE DRAGON**, LOVESWEPT #892. With only a book and an ancient ring to guide her, Lydia

Star falls back in time and lands at the feet of a fire-breathing dragon. Lydia is saved by one of King Arthur's brave knights, Sir Dragon, and is forced to face the fact that she's not in San Diego anymore. Dragon is bewildered by his mysterious prisoner, but can't help being captivated by her ethereal beauty. Convinced that she is the result of some deviltry, he confides in the king's counsel, Merlyn. Lydia knows her time is running out and longs for the comforts of home, a fact that keeps her trying desperately to escape from the overbearing knight's clutches. Can this warrior be the keeper of her soul? Better yet, will he survive the journey to his heart's true home? Peggy Webb more than answers these questions with this sensual dream of a romance.

Catherine Mulvany treats us to **AQUAMARINE**, LOVESWEPT #893. Teague Harris can't believe his eyes when he sees his supposedly dead fiancée walking around the carnival grounds. He's even more surprised when he realizes that Shea McKenzie might not be his former love . . . but she does look enough like Kirsten Rainey to pose as the missing heiress for Kirsten's dying father. Drawn to Idaho by a postcard found among her dead mother's things, Shea reluctantly agrees to the outrageous masquerade after seeing a picture of a man who could pass for her own father. Then, as Shea discovers a cluster of glowing aquamarine crystals, she begins to experience Kirsten's memories. Can Shea trust Teague, a man who seems more interested in trying to solve the murder of Shea's twin than in moving on with the rest of his life? Catherine Mulvany teaches us that love is the strongest force on earth!

Happy reading!

With warmest wishes,

Susann Brailey   Joy Abella

Susann Brailey   Joy Abella

Senior Editor   Administrative Editor

P.S. Look for these women's fiction titles coming in June! From Nora Roberts comes **GENUINE LIES**, now in hardcover for the first time ever. Hollywood legend Eve Benedict selects Julia Summers to write her biography. Sparks fly and danger looms as three Hollywood players attempt to protect what they value most. Talented author Jane Feather introduces an irresistible new trilogy, beginning with **THE HOSTAGE BRIDE**. Three girls make a pact never to get married, but when Portia is accidentally kidnapped by a gang of outlaws, her hijacker gets more than he bargained for in his defiant and surprisingly attractive captive. And finally, Rebecca Kelley presents her debut, **THE WEDDING CHASE**. Zel Fleetwood is looking for a wealthy husband who can save her family. Instead she attracts the unwanted attentions of the earl of Northcliffe, whose ardent but misguided interest ruins her prospects. That is, until he realizes *he*'s the perfect match for her. And immediately following this page, preview the Bantam women's fiction titles on sale in May!

For current information on Bantam's women's fiction, visit our Web site at the following address:
http://www.bdd.com/romance

Don't miss these extraordinary novels from Bantam Books!

On sale in May:

A PLACE TO CALL HOME
by Deborah Smith

THE WITCH AND THE WARRIOR
by Karyn Monk

Come home to the best-loved novel
of the year . . .

A Place to Call Home
BY DEBORAH SMITH

Twenty years ago, Claire Maloney was the willful, pampered, tomboyish daughter of the town's most respected family, but that didn't stop her from befriending Roan Sullivan, a fierce, motherless boy who lived in a rusted-out trailer amid junked cars. No one in Dunderry, Georgia—least of all Claire's family—could understand the bond between these two mavericks. But Roan and Claire belonged together . . . until the dark afternoon when violence and terror overtook them, and Roan disappeared from Claire's life. Now, two decades later, Claire is adrift, and the Maloneys are still hoping the past can be buried under the rich Southern soil. But Roan Sullivan is about to walk back into their lives. . . . By turns tender and sexy and heartbreaking and exuberant, A Place to Call Home *is an enthralling journey between two hearts—and a deliciously original novel from one of the most imaginative and appealing new voices in Southern fiction.*

"A beautiful, believable love story."
—*Chicago Tribune*

It started the year I performed as a tap-dancing leprechaun at the St. Patrick's Day carnival and Roanie Sullivan threatened to cut my cousin Carlton's throat with a rusty pocketknife. That was also the year the Beatles broke up and the National Guard killed four students at

Kent State, and Josh, who was in Vietnam, wrote home to Brady, who was a senior at Dunderry High, *Don't even think about enlisting. There's nothing patriotic about this shit.*

But I was only five years old; my world was narrow, deep, self-satisfied, well-off, very Southern, securely bound to the land and to a huge family descended almost entirely from Irish immigrants who had settled in the Georgia mountains over one hundred and thirty years ago. As far as I was concerned, life revolved in simple circles with me at the center.

The St. Patrick's Day carnival was nothing like it is now. There were no tents set up to dispense green beer, no artists selling handmade 24-karat-gold shamrock jewelry, no Luck of the Irish 5K Road Race, no imported musicians playing authentic Irish jigs on the town square. Now it's a *festival*, one of the top tourist events in the state.

But when I was five it was just a carnival, held in the old Methodist campground arbor east of town. The Jaycees and the Dunderry Ladies' Association sold barbecue sandwiches, green sugar cookes, and lime punch at folding tables in a corner next to the arbor's wooden stage, the Down Mountain Boys played bluegrass music, and the beginners' tap class from my Aunt Gloria's School of Dance was decked out in leprechaun costumes and forced into a mid-year minirecital.

Mama took snapshots of me in my involuntary servitude. I was not a born dancer. I had no rhythm, I was always out of step, and I disliked mastering anyone's routines but my own. I stood there on the stage, staring resolutely at the camera in my green-checkered bibbed dress with its ruffled skirt and a puffy white blouse, my green socks and black patent-leather tap shoes with green bows, my hair parted in fat red braids tied with green ribbons.

I looked like an unhappy Irish Heidi.

My class, all twenty of us, stomped and shuffled through our last number, accompanied by a tune from some Irish dance record I don't remember, which Aunt Gloria played full blast on her portable stereo connected to the Down Mountain Boys' big amplifiers. I looked down and there he was, standing in the crowd at the lip of the stage, a tall, shabby, ten-year-old boy with greasy black hair. Roan Sullivan. *Roanie.* Even in a small town the levels of society are a steep staircase. My family was at the top. Roan and his daddy weren't just at the bottom; they were in the cellar.

He watched me seriously, as if I weren't making a fool of myself, which I was. I had already accidentally stomped on my cousin Violet's left foot twice, and I'd elbowed my cousin Rebecca in her right arm, so they'd given me a wide berth on either side.

I forgot about my humiliating arms and feet and concentrated on Roanie Sullivan avidly, because it was the first close look I'd gotten at nasty, no-account Big Roan Sullivan's son from Sullivan's Hollow. We didn't associate with Big Roan Sullivan, even though he and Roanie were our closest neighbors on Soap Falls Road. The Hollow might as well have been on the far side of China, not two miles from our farm.

"That godforsaken hole only produces one thing—*trash.*" That's what Uncle Pete and Uncle Bert always said about the Hollow. And because everybody knew Roanie Sullivan was trash—came from it, looked like it, and smelled like it—they steered clear of him in the crowd. Maybe that was one reason I couldn't take my eyes off him. We were both human islands stuck in the middle of a lonely, embarrassing sea of space.

My cousin Carlton lounged a couple of feet away, between Roanie and the Jaycees' table. There are some relatives you just tolerate, and Carlton Maloney was in that group. He was about twelve, smug and well-fed, and he was laughing at me so hard that his eyes nearly disappeared in his face. He and my brother Hop were in the seventh grade together. Hop said he cheated on math tests. He was a weasel.

I saw him glance behind him. Once, twice. Uncle Dwayne was in charge of the Jaycees' food table and Aunt Rhonda was talking to him about something, so he was looking at her dutifully. He'd left a couple of dollar bills beside the cardboard shoe box he was using as a cash till.

Carlton eased one hand over, snatched the money, and stuck it in his trouser pocket.

I was stunned. He'd stolen from the Jaycees. He'd stolen from his own *uncle*. My brothers and I had been trained to such a strict code of honor that we wouldn't pilfer so much as a penny from the change cup on Daddy's dresser. I admit I had a weakness for the bags of chocolate chips in the bakery section of the grocery store, and if one just *happened* to fall off the shelf and burst open, I'd sample a few. But nonedible property was sacred. And stealing *money* was unthinkable.

Uncle Dwayne looked down at the table. He frowned. He hunted among packages of sugar cookies wrapped in cellophane and tied with green ribbons. He leaned toward Carlton and said something to him. From the stage I couldn't hear what he said—I couldn't hear anything except the music pounding in my ears—but I saw Carlton draw back dramatically, shaking his head. Then he turned and pointed at Roanie.

I was struck tapless. I simply couldn't move a foot. I stood there, rooted in place, and was dimly, painfully aware of people laughing at me, of my grandparents hiding their smiles behind their hands, and of Mama's and

Daddy's bewildered stares. Daddy, who could not dance either, waved his big hands helpfully, as if I was a scared calf he could shoo into moving again.

But I wasn't scared. I was furious.

Uncle Dwayne, his jaw thrust out, pushed his way around the table and grabbed Roanie by one arm. I saw Uncle Dwayne speak forcefully to him. I saw the blank expression on Roanie's face turn to sullen anger. I guess it wasn't the first time he'd been accused of something he didn't do.

His eyes darted to Carlton. He lunged at him. They went down in a heap, with Carlton on the bottom. People scattered, yelling. The whole Leprechaun Review came to a wobbly halt. Aunt Gloria bounded to her portable record player and the music ended with a screech like an amplified zipper. I bolted down the stairs at that end of the stage and squirmed through the crowd of adults.

Uncle Dwayne was trying to pull Roanie off Carlton, but Roanie had one hand wound in the collar of Carlton's sweater. He had the other at Carlton's throat, with the point of a rusty little penknife poised beneath Carlton's Adam's apple. "I didn't take no money!" Roanie yelled at him. "You damn liar!"

Daddy plowed into the action. He planted a knee in Roanie's back and wrenched the knife out of his hand. He and Uncle Dwayne pried the boys apart, and Daddy pulled Roanie to his feet. "He has a knife," I heard someone whisper. "That Sullivan boy's vicious."

"Where's that money?" Uncle Dwayne thundered, peering down into Roanie Sullivan's face. "Give it to me. Right now."

"I ain't got no money. I didn't take no money." He mouthed words like a hillbilly, kind of honking them out half finished. He had a crooked front tooth with jagged edges, too. It flashed like a lopsided fang.

"Oh, yeah, you did," Carlton yelled. "I saw you! Everybody knows you steal stuff! Just like your daddy!"

"Roanie, hand over the money," Daddy said. Daddy had a booming voice. He was fair, but he was tough. "Don't make me go through your pockets," he added sternly. "Come on, boy, tell the truth and give the money back."

"I ain't *got* it."

I was plastered to the sidelines but close enough to see the misery and defensiveness in Roanie's face. Oh, lord. He was the kind of boy who fought and cussed and put a knife to people's throats. He caused trouble. He deserved trouble.

But he's not a thief.

Don't tattle on Carlton. Maloneys stick together. We're big, that way.

But it's not fair.

"All right, Roanie," Daddy said, and reached for the back pocket of Roanie's dirty jeans.

"He didn't take it," I said loudly. "Carlton did!" Everyone stared at me. Well, I'd gotten used to that. I met Roanie Sullivan's wary, surprised eyes. He could burn a hole through me with those eyes.

Uncle Dwayne glared at me. "Now, Claire. Are you sure you're not getting back at Carlton because he spit boiled peanuts at you outside Sunday school last week?"

No, but I knew how a boiled peanut felt. Hot, real hot. "Roanie didn't take the money," I repeated. I jabbed a finger at Carlton. "Carlton did. I *saw* him, Daddy. I saw him stick it in his front pocket."

Daddy and Uncle Dwayne pivoted slowly. Carlton's face, already sweaty and red, turned crimson. "*Carlton,*" Uncle Dwayne said.

"She's just picking on me!"

Uncle Dwayne stuck a hand in Carlton's pocket and pulled out two wadded-up dollar bills.

And that was that.

Uncle Dwayne hauled Carlton off to find Uncle Eugene and Aunt Arnetta, Carlton's folks. Daddy let go of Roanie Sullivan. "Go on. Get out of here."

"He pulled that knife, Holt," Uncle Pete said behind me.

Daddy scowled. "He couldn't cut his way out of a paper sack with a knife that little."

"But he *pulled* it on Carlton."

"Forget about it, Pete. Go on, everybody."

Roanie stared at me. I held his gaze as if hypnotized. Isolation radiated from him like an invisible shield, but there was this *gleam* in his eyes, made up of surprise and gratitude and suspicion, bearing on me like concentrated fire, and I felt singed. Daddy put a hand on the collar of the faded, floppy football jersey he wore and dragged him away. I started to follow, but Mama had gotten through the crowd by then, and she snagged me by the back of my dress. "Hold on, Claire Karleen Maloney. You've put on enough of a show."

Dazed, I looked up at her. Hop and Evan peered at me from her side. Violet and Rebecca watched me, open-mouthed. A whole bunch of Maloneys scrutinized me. "Carlton's a weasel," I explained finally.

Mama nodded. "You told the truth. That's fine. You're done. I'm proud of you."

"Then how come everybody's lookin' at me like I'm weird?"

"Because you *are*," Rebecca blurted out. "Aren't you scared of Roanie Sullivan?"

"He didn't laugh at me when I was dancing. I think he's okay."

"You've got a strange way of sortin' things out," Evan said.

"She's one brick short of a load," Hop added.

So that was the year I realized Roanie was not just trashy, not just different, he was dangerous, and taking his side was a surefire way to seed my own mild reputation as a troublemaker and Independent Thinker.

I was fascinated by him from then on.

"An enthralling tale of two compelling, heartwarming characters and the healing power of love . . . I loved it!"—Elizabeth Thornton, author of *You Only Love Twice*

The historical tales of Karyn Monk are filled with unforgettable romance and her own special brand of warmth and humor. Now love casts its spell in the Highlands, as a warrior seeks a miracle from a mysterious lady of secrets and magic. . . .

The Witch and the Warrior

BY KARYN MONK

Suspected of witchcraft, Gwendolyn MacSween has been condemned to being burned at the stake at the hands of her own clan. Yet rescue comes from a most unlikely source. Mad Alex MacDunn, laird of the mighty rival clan MacDunn, is a man whose past is scarred with tragedy and loss. His last hope lies in capturing the witch of the MacSweens—and using her magic to heal his dying son. He expects to find an old hag. . . . Instead he finds a young woman of unearthly beauty. There's only one problem: Gwendolyn has no power to bewitch or to heal. Now she must pretend to be a sorceress—or herself perish. But can she use her common sense to save Alex's son, and her natural powers as a woman to enchant a fierce and handsome Highland warrior—before a dangerous enemy destroys them both?

Gwendolyn regarded the sky in bewilderment. She had never witnessed such an abrupt change in the weather.

"Everything is fine," she assured them loudly. "The spirits have heard my plea."

They remained in their circle, watching the sky as a cool gale whipped their hair and clothes. And then, just as suddenly as it burst upon them, the storm died. The wind gasped and was gone, and the clouds melted into the darkness, unveiling the silent, tranquil glow of the moon and stars once again.

"By God, that was something!" roared Cameron, slapping Brodick heartily on the back. "Have you ever seen such a thing?"

"Did you see that, Alex?" demanded Brodick, looking uneasy.

"Aye," said Alex. "I saw."

Brodick raised his arm and cautiously flexed it at the elbow. "I think my arm feels better." He sounded more troubled than pleased.

"I *know* my head feels better!" said Cameron happily. "What about you, Neddie?"

"I have no wounds for the witch to heal," said Ned, shrugging. He frowned, then shrugged again. "That's odd," he remarked, slowly turning his head from side to side. "My neck has been stiff and aching for a week, and suddenly it feels fine."

Gwendolyn folded her arms across her chest and regarded them triumphantly. Clearly just the suggestion that they would feel better had had an effect on them, which was what she had hoped would happen. Luckily, the weather had complemented her little performance.

"Can you cast that spell on anyone?" asked Cameron, still excited.

"Not everyone," she replied carefully. "And my spells don't always work."

"What do you mean?" demanded Alex.

"The success of a spell depends on many things," she replied evasively. She did not want him to think she could simply say a few words and fell an entire army. "My powers will not work on everyone."

"I don't give a damn if they work on everyone," he growled. "As long as they work on one person." His expression was harsh. "Cameron, take the first watch. The rest of you get some sleep. We ride at first light."

Brodick produced an extra plaid from his horse and carefully draped it over Isabella's unconscious form. Then he lay down just a few feet away from her, where he could watch over her during the night. Ned and MacDunn also stretched out upon the ground, arranging part of their plaids over their shoulders for warmth.

"Do you sleep standing up?" MacDunn asked irritably.

"No," replied Gwendolyn.

"Then lie down," he orderd. "We still have a long journey ahead."

She had assumed they were going to bind her to a tree. But with Cameron watching her, she would not get very far if she attempted to escape tonight. Obviously that was what MacDunn believed. Relieved that she would not be tied, she wearily lowered herself to the ground.

Tomorrow would be soon enough to find an opportunity for escape.

The little camp grew quiet, except for the occasional snap of the fire. Soon the rumble of snoring began to drift lazily through the air. Gwendolyn wondered how they had all managed to find sleep so quickly in such uncomfortable conditions. The fire had died and the ground was damp and cold, forcing her to curl into a tight ball and wrap her bare arms around herself. It didn't help. With every passing moment her flesh grew more chilled, until finally her entire body was shivering uncontrollably.

"Gwendolyn," called MacDunn in a low voice, "come here."

She sat up and peered at him through the darkness. "Why?" she demanded suspiciously.

"Because your chattering teeth are keeping me awake," he grumbled. "You will lie next to me and share my plaid."

She stared at him in horror. "I am fine, MacDunn," she hastily assured him. "You needn't concern yourself about—"

"Come here," he repeated firmly.

"No," she replied, shaking her head. "I may be your prisoner, but I will *not* share your bed."

She waited for him to argue. Instead he muttered something under his breath, adjusted his plaid more to his liking over his naked chest and closed his eyes once again. Satisfied that she had won this small but critical battle, she vigorously rubbed her arms to warm them, then primly curled onto the ground.

Her teeth began to chatter so violently she had to bite down hard to try to control them.

The next thing she knew, MacDunn was stretching out beside her and wrapping his plaid over both of them.

"Don't you dare touch me!" Gwendolyn hissed, rolling away.

MacDunn grabbed her waist and firmly drew her back, imprisoning her in the warm crook of his enormous, barely clad body.

"Be still!" he ordered impatiently.

"I will not be still, you foul, mad ravisher of women!" She kicked him as hard as she could in his shin.

"Jesus—" he swore, loosening his hold slightly.

Gwendolyn tried to scramble away from him, but he instantly tightened his grip.

"Listen to me!" he commanded, somehow managing to keep his voice low. "I have no intention of bedding you, do you understand?"

Gwendolyn glared at him, her breasts rising and falling so rapidly they grazed his bandaged chest.

"I may be considered mad," he continued, "but to my knowledge I have not yet earned a reputation as a ravager of unwilling women—do you understand?"

His blue eyes held hers. She tried to detect deceit in them, but could not. All she saw was anger, mingled with weariness.

"I have already risked far more than I have a right to, to save your life and take you home with me, Gwendolyn MacSween," he continued. "I will *not* have it end by watching you fall deathly ill from the chill of the night."

He waited a moment, allowing his comments to penetrate her fear. Then, cautiously, he loosened his grip. "Lie still," he ordered gruffly. "I will keep you warm, nothing more. You have my word."

She regarded him warily. "You swear you will not abuse me, MacDunn? On your honor?"

"I swear."

Reluctantly, she eased herself onto her side. MacDunn adjusted part of his plaid over her, then once again fitted himself around her. His arm circled her waist, drawing her into the warm, hard cradle of his body. Gwendolyn lay there rigidly for a long while, scarcely breathing, waiting for him to break his word.

Instead, he began to snore.

Heat seemed to radiate from him, slowly permeating

her chilled flesh. It warmed even the soft wool of his plaid, she realized, snuggling further into it. A deliciously masculine scent wafted around her, the scent of horse and leather and woods. Little by little, the feel of MacDunn's powerful body against hers became more comforting than threatening, especially as his snores grew louder.

Until that moment, she had had virtually no knowledge of physical contact. Her mother had died when she was very young, and her father, though loving, had never been at ease with open demonstrations of affection. The unfamiliar sensation of MacDunn's warm body wrapped protectively around her was unlike anything she had ever imagined. She was his prisoner. And yet, she felt impossibly safe.

"You belong to me now," he had told her. *"I protect what is mine."* She belonged to no one. She reflected drowsily, and no one could protect her from men like Robert, or the ignorance and fear that was sure to fester in MacDunn's own clan the moment they saw her. She would escape him long before they reached his lands. Tomorrow, she would break free from these warriors, so she could retrieve the stone, return to her clan and kill Robert. Above all else, Robert must die. She would make him pay for murdering her father and destroying her life.

But all this seemed distant and shadowy as she drifted into slumber, sheltered by this brave, mad warrior, whose heart pulsed steadily against her back.

On sale in June:

GENUINE LIES
by Nora Roberts

THE HOSTAGE BRIDE
by Jane Feather

THE WEDDING CHASE
by Rebecca Kelley

Bestselling Historical Women's Fiction

⚮ AMANDA QUICK ⚮

____28354-5 SEDUCTION . . .$6.50/$8.99 Canada

____28932-2 SCANDAL . . . .$6.50/$8.99

____28594-7 SURRENDER . . . .$6.50/$8.99

____29325-7 RENDEZVOUS . . . .$6.50/$8.99

____29315-X RECKLESS . . . .$6.50/$8.99

____29316-8 RAVISHED . . . .$6.50/$8.99

____29317-6 DANGEROUS . . . .$6.50/$8.99

____56506-0 DECEPTION . . . .$6.50/$8.99

____56153-7 DESIRE . . . .$6.50/$8.99

____56940-6 MISTRESS . . . .$6.50/$8.99

____57159-1 MYSTIQUE . . . .$6.50/$7.99

____57190-7 MISCHIEF . . . .$6.50/$8.99

____57407-8 AFFAIR . . . .$6.99/$8.99

⚮ IRIS JOHANSEN ⚮

____29871-2 LAST BRIDGE HOME . . .$5.50/$7.50

____29604-3 THE GOLDEN
                    BARBARIAN . . . .$6.99/$8.99

____29244-7 REAP THE WIND . . . . . .$5.99/$7.50

____29032-0 STORM WINDS . . . .$6.99/$8.99

Ask for these books at your local bookstore or use this page to order.

Please send me the books I have checked above. I am enclosing $____ (add $2.50 to cover postage and handling). Send check or money order, no cash or C.O.D.'s, please.

Name _____

Address _____

City/State/Zip _____

Send order to: Bantam Books, Dept. FN 16, 2451 S. Wolf Rd., Des Plaines, IL 60018
Allow four to six weeks for delivery.
Prices and availability subject to change without notice.   FN 16 3/98

Bestselling Historical Women's Fiction

⚘ IRIS JOHANSEN ⚘

⚘ TERESA MEDEIROS ⚘

- - - - - - - - - - - - - - - - - - - -

Ask for these books at your local bookstore or use this page to order.

Please send me the books I have checked above. I am enclosing $____ (add $2.50 to cover postage and handling). Send check or money order, no cash or C.O.D.'s, please.

Name _____

Address _____

City/State/Zip _____

Send order to: Bantam Books, Dept. FN 16, 2451 S. Wolf Rd., Des Plaines, IL 60018
Allow four to six weeks for delivery.
Prices and availability subject to change without notice.   FN 16 3/98